Lady Georgiana Fullerton

Rosemary

A Tale of the Fire of London

Lady Georgiana Fullerton

Rosemary
A Tale of the Fire of London

ISBN/EAN: 9783337242596

Printed in Europe, USA, Canada, Australia, Japan

Cover: Foto ©Andreas Hilbeck / pixelio.de

More available books at **www.hansebooks.com**

ROSEMARY;

A TALE OF THE FIRE OF LONDON.

BY

LADY GEORGIANA FULLERTON.

————

NEW YORK:
P. O'SHEA, PUBLISHER,
37 BARCLAY STREET AND 42 PARK PLACE.
1874.

CONTENTS.

———

ROSEMARY.

A TALE OF THE FIRE OF LONDON.

CHAPTER I.

WISHING SOMETHING TO HAPPEN—SOMETHING
HAPPENS.

IN a small house in London, close to the old
Westminster Bridge, there lived, rather more
than two hundred years ago, a good old lady,
commonly called the Widow Coggle. She and
her maid, Joan Porter, had inhabited this little
house for a quarter of a century; that is, since
the death of Mr. Coggle; and though they had
disputed daily during all that time on every
possible subject within their narrow reach, they
had never quarrelled, and neither of them would
probably have been able to exist comfortably
without the other.

On the day on which this story begins, Mrs.
Coggle was sitting at her work-table with a dis-
consolately wistful expression of countenance,
which betokened an unsatisfied state of mind
and a desire to complain of something or of
somebody.   Which of these two alternatives
gives the greatest relief to persons laboring
under that sort of craving, it would be difficult
to decide; there is much to be said on both
sides.   In complaining of things, troublesome
scruples do not often arise.   People say, " This
odious weather ! " or " This horrid pen ! " or
" This dreadful table ! " or " Those abominable
tongs ! " without any remorse ; whereas if they
exclaim, " That odious Mrs. John ! " or " That
horrid Mr. James ! " or " That dreadful Miss
Thomas ! " or " That abominable Sarah ! " they
are apt, if ever so little accustomed to examine
their consciences, to feel a little uncomfortable
shortly afterwards.   They are obliged to
modify those adjectives, and to describe their
acquaintances as only tiresome and disagree-
able, and enough to provoke a saint.   Such
restraint no doubt interferes with the relief

afforded by the thorough-going expressions fearlessly applied to the table or to the tongs. But then, on the other hand, the passiveness of those latter objects—the unimpressionable way in which they remain unconscious of the abuse they receive—reacts unpleasantly on the excited state of feelings which originates it, and necessarily prevents the continuance of the outbursts which, when addressed to a human being, can be indefinitely prolonged with more or less present satisfaction, though at the risk of subsequent uneasiness.

Mrs. Coggle, the lady who lived in London two centuries ago, had probably never deeply considered that question, and acted impulsively on the subject. As she pulled off her spectacles and exclaimed, "They grows dimmer and dimmer every day!" or when her needle dropped out of her fingers on the floor, declared needles in general to be "the most plaguing, sticking-in-all-directions, and getting-out-of-the-way things in the world," there was probably in her mind a sort of idea that if Joan Porter would but come home her internal condition would improve. She should scold Joan, or Joan would take her to task; things would not remain just as they were. The fact was that the state of the weather was at the bottom of Mrs. Coggle's state of mind. She had set her heart on going to sup that day with Mrs. Biddle, Mr. Yates's housekeeper. Her husband had been a draper, and supplied wealthy houses in his day, and she had in consequence a sort of acquaintanceship with many families amongst the London gentry, especially amongst those that had not at all, or only recently, conformed to the times. She was herself a Catholic, but not a confessor or a candidate for martyrdom; and it had been for the many years they had lived together one of the principal subjects of dispute between her and Joan Porter what degree of conformity to the times was allowable under the circumstances. Mr. George Yates's deceased parents had been some of the best customers of the late Mr. Coggle, and the young couple, who had now succeeded to their fortune, continued to show kindness to his widow. As to Joan Porter, she was a well-known character in those days; had helped many a Catholic family out of a difficulty; saved many a priest from arrest; and, under an eccentric simplicity of mind and manner, concealed much shrewdness.

Three weeks before the day on which Mrs Coggle wanted it to be fine, and it would rain, Mrs. Yates had been confined of a little girl, and this was one of the reasons why the draper's widow was anxious to keep her engagement with Mrs. Biddle. She had seen Mrs. Yates herself in her cradle when she was only a few days old, and she should not like it to be said she had not seen little Missy before other folk had had a sight of her. But if it rained—at that moment the door opened, and Joan Porter entered the room in a nondescript costume, the most remarkable feature of which was a red-and-yellow handkerchief tied round something that looked very like a white nightcap, and holding in her hands an umbrella such as Sisters of St. Vincent of Paul use nowadays — gray, heavy, and solid-looking.

" Well, ma'am, people say it never rains but it

pours, which I could never see myself to be true; but if it never poured before, I do warrant you it does so at this here blessed minute."

"It always does rain, Joan, when I've set my heart on something."

"Then, ma'am," Joan replied, as she spread the umbrella to dry, which it began to do by making a circle of little ponds on the floor— "then, ma'am, if that be the reason that it rains, why does you go on setting your heart on things, if so be you want it to be fine?"

"I really think, Joan, if you was to lend me your umbrella—"

"Laws, ma'am, and who's to carry it over your head? You have no more strength to do it yourself than a new-born babe."

"It's just a new-born babe I want for to go and see—Mrs. Yates's, as was born three weeks ago."

Joan shrugged her shoulders with unutterable contempt.

"Well, ma'am, I thought you was older and wiser than that; to go for to get wet, and catch

the rheumatics and the Lord knows what besides, just for to look at a baby ! Babies be as
plentiful as blackberries. I'm sure *I* would not
go out of my way to see twenty of them, if you
should pay me for it."

"O, I dare say not," Mrs. Coggle answered
sarcastically. "You'd think more of Mrs. Biddle's cakes and her cowslip wine than of the
little stranger. Mrs. Yates always sends me
something nice from her own table when I sups
at her house, and if I meet her on the stairs she
speaks as civil as possible."

"O, as to that, ma'am, I don't go for to say
anything against Mrs. Yates, or cakes, or civil-
ity, or little strangers. It's going out for to see
them when it's a wet dripping night, enough to
soak the rheumatism into your bones, that I calls
fudge."

Mrs. Coggle sighed deeply, and resumed her
work ; and in a few minutes said, in a senten-
tious manner, " What makes me so partial to
new-born babes, Joan, is that they be so innocent."

"They be not so innocent always as they

looks," Joan retorted. "They go into dreadful passions if you contradicts them."

" To hear you talk folks would think you had never been a baby yourself."

"Well, I may have been, or I mayn't; anyways, I don't recollect anything about it. Do you, ma'am, remember being a baby?"

"Of course I do," Mrs. Coggle answered; then, correcting herself, added, " that is, when I look at that picture of myself, with a rose in my hand, a sitting on my mother's knees."

" O, ay, that pink-cheeked wench over the chimney. I sometimes sits and wonders to think that was you, ma'am. She's got such a pretty face, that little minx."

Mrs. Coggle felt rather nettled at the inference contained in this last speech of Joan's. "Grown people, I suppose, may be handsome, though not pink-cheeked like babies?"

" I didn't say they couldn't. 'Handsome is as handsome does,' and you does very handsome things, ma'am. I'm sure that patchwork quilt on the bed up-stairs is as handsome a one as can be seen. Mrs. Dimple says so."

The conversation was now arriving at that point where Mrs. Coggle always found a difficulty in arguing with Joan, and when it touched upon a personal matter was apt to become irritable.

" Well now, Joan," she exclaimed, " I should like to know, once for all, be you a fool or be you not?"

" That's just as you like to take me, ma'am ; you ought to know best, I have lived with you so long."

" I cannot go for to make up my mind," Mrs. Coggle said, in the same tone of cutting sarcasm.

" Nor I, ma'am," Joan rejoined, " for so long as I have knowed myself. You see, wise people do be sometimes so like fools, and fools so like wise people, 'tis hard to tell."

" What do you know about wise people?"

Joan's eyes twinkled with a funny expression, as she replied,

" Laws, ma'am! does not I know you?"

" Then do you mean to say I am like a fool?"

"O dear, dear, I never thought of that, I'm sure; but 'ceptions makes the rule, you know."

"Now, Joan, what do you mean by that?"

"That you're the 'ception, ma'am, and I'm the rule."

"Well, you had better hold your tongue, Joan, if you can't talk more to the purpose."

Mrs. Coggle often ended in that manner her conversations with Joan, who was more willing in the long run to remain silent than her mistress.

The day was waning, and the dull heavy twilight gradually disappearing. Here and there, amongst the thick murky clouds which were rapidly driven over the face of the sky, a star began to glimmer, and lights to be seen on the banks of the river and the barges with which they were lined. It was still raining, but the wind was beginning to rise, and there seemed a prospect of the night clearing. No sound was heard in the little parlor, which was getting very dark, save the ticking of the clock, and now and then a yawn.

At last Mrs. Coggle, wearied of the inactivity of her hands and of her tongue, said,

"I am that bored that I should like something to happen."

"To you or to me, ma'am?" Joan inquired.

"Not to any one in particular, you foolish creature."

"What, to every one at once, ma'am? That would be worse, I take it, for then there would be nobody to help nobody."

"Didn't I tell you to hold your tongue, Joan?" the widow said, in an aggrieved tone of voice.

"Yes, ma'am," Joan answered, "but that was before you wanted something to happen. I suppose," she added, "that it's time now to shut the shutters and light the candle. It can't be noways darker than it is now." As she said this, Joan went to the window. "O my good God!" she exclaimed.

"What, Joan, what?" cried Mrs. Coggle, stumbling over the footstool on her way to the window.

"O good Lord! if there's not something in-

deed happening now on t'other side of the river,
Jesu, Mary, what a red light! O laws, what a
blaze! O, what a frightful fire! Mercy on us!"
Joan crossed herself, and then stood silently
gazing at the awful spectacle, her lips moving
as if in prayer.

Not so Mrs. Coggle, who, when she caught
sight of the fire, remained one instant as if
petrified, and then began to scream as if she
was herself surrounded by the flames.

"O Joan, Joan, what shall we do?"

"Do! Why, do nothing, ma'am; there's
the river between us and the fire anyways."

"O, it be so dreadful! Get me some brandy,
I shall faint." And suiting the action to the
word, Mrs. Coggle let herself gently fall on the
floor; but only for a moment. Starting up
again, and clinging to Joan, she cried, "Let us
run and pack up our clothes. Where are the
keys? We shall be burnt in our beds."

"No, ma'am, we won't get into our beds, and
then we can't be burnt in them. But, bless
your soul—what's the use of pulling your cap
off? Your wig is coming off too."

This suggestion turned the current of the widow's thoughts for a moment, while she was restoring the endangered wig to its place. Joan, with her eyes fixed on the river, which the conflagration was now illuminating with a terrible glare, clasped her hands together, and from her quivering lips words such as these broke from time to time:

"They are getting into boats them as have jumped out of the windows. O, how they scream! I'll tell you what, ma'am, it will be next door to a miracle if all London ain't burnt to-morrow!"

CHAPTER II.

VISITORS.

JOAN'S previsions proved in a measure correct. Neither a miracle nor anything next door to it took place. The fire which was to devour a great portion of old London, and reduce to ashes many of its great edifices as well as thousands of its close-built wooden houses, continued to rage with unabating violence.

Great was the ruin wrought and the desolation caused by that fearful conflagration. Many a precious life was lost, many a happy home suddenly annihilated. Who can reckon the number of vanished joys, of blighted hopes, and broken hearts which such a catastrophe leaves behind it? Public events of such magnitude, whilst they strike the world with awe, influence many an obscure destiny on which it does not bestow a thought.

The fire of London had a great deal to do

with the fate of the little Missy whom Mrs. Coggle had so much wished to look at in her cradle. But as she watched the progress of the flames it did not even occur to her what an escape she had had that evening, and how fortunate it had been that the rain had kept her at home on the safe side of the river. Both she and Joan stood riveted to the same spot, shivering and trembling, especially at the rushing sound of feet and the screams in the narrow street at the backside of the house. Mrs. Coggle repeated once or twice her attempt at fainting; but it did not succeed. Excitement and curiosity impeded the collapse. Joan went on saying her prayers, and when a crash louder than usual indicated that some building was falling, she thought of the souls that might be at that moment passing into eternity, and devoutly crossing herself she murmured, "God ha' mercy on them."

All at once a loud knocking was heard at the door.

"Bless my soul," Mrs. Coggle exclaimed, "who, in the name of wonder, can that be at

this time of the night? I'm that frightened l
cannot move. For Heaven's sake, Joan, look
who they be before you open the door."

As there was no way of peeping except
through the key-hole, and it was too dark to see
anything, Joan could not well comply with this
command, but she said, with an expressive
shrug,

"I know them by their voices. It's those
women, Mrs. Peterkin and Mrs. Crump. They
always run in couples, and whatever happens
they turns up."

So saying, she opened the door, and the two
individuals she had named rushed in.

"O neighbor! neighbor!" Mrs. Peterkin exclaimed.

"O Mistress Coggle, Mistress Coggle," Mrs.
Crump cried.

And then Mrs. Peterkin broke forth in a
pathetic tone, "What are you made of, ma'am,
that you can be looking quietly out of window,
and London burning all the time?"

"That's just what I've been saying to Joan,"
Mrs. Coggle answered, in an aggrieved voice;

"I wanted to go out, didn't I, Joan, and you prevented me? Who ever heard of such a thing as staying at home when London was on fire! Give me my cloak, Joan."

"No, ma'am, you sha'nt stir out; leastways, not till the Thames catches fire, and those good ladies, I'm thinking, won't be those to set it burning. Now, do you sit down, mistress, like a sensible Christian woman, and let other folks make fools of themselves, if so be it pleases them. Much good it will do to the poor creatures yonder if you gets yourself trodden to death by the crowd!"

Mrs. Peterkin thought this remark a very heartless one, and said some people had no feelings; upon which Joan observed that she had a feeling as how she would like to see Mrs. Peterkin mind her own business and leave her mistress alone. A sharp altercation might have followed, not the first between those two combatants, if at that moment the burning rafters of a large house on the opposite bank had not given way with a fearful glare, and made the whole scene clearly visible.

2

"'Tis like the Day of Judgment!" Mrs Crump exclaimed, and began to scream.

"In that ere case you'd better say your prayers, and not 'wilder other folks with shrieking," Joan observed.

This remark checked for a moment the outburst of Mrs. Crump's feeling, and during the pause that ensued Mrs. Peterkin uttered the following words in an oracular tone of voice.

"I'll warrant you, ladies, that it's the Papists have done it. I always said they would burn us in our beds."

This mention of beds touched Mrs. Coggle to the quick.

"O dear! O dear!" she cried, wringing her hands. "Joan says we mustn't go to bed no more. To think we should come to that!"

"Never you mind, mistress. You'll go to bed till you are tired of it, if you will only sit still a bit."

Having administered these words of consolation to her mistress, Joan turned with a severe aspect toward Mrs. Peterkin.

"If you please, ma'am, will you keep a civil

tongue in your head when you speak of Papists, as you calls them, and not go for to go and put about such big lies about them?"

"O my goodness, Mrs. Coggle! I say, Mrs. Crump, did you ever hear the like of that?"

Mrs. Crump never had, nor Mrs. Coggle either. The former had, however, no inclination at that moment to take up the cudgels on either side, and she exclaimed,

"But I say, neighbor, I'm not going to stop here doing nothing. This is a sight folks may'nt live to see twice in their lives. Come, let us run—run."

Joan closed the door on the departing visitors, and when, on returning to the window, she caught sight of them a moment afterwards flying across the bridge, she relieved herself by ejaculating:

"The two silly creatures! There they go, tearing away amongst the crowd like demented persons. I should like to clap them both into Bedlam."

Then turning to her mistress, she said,

"Well, ma'am, I hopes you'll never again

wish something to happen! For my part, I
think it's next door to a sin."

Quite crestfallen, Mrs. Coggle did not attempt
to justify her unlucky desire; but sinking down
in her easy chair, declared she should never get
over it. As to going to bed, she should never
think of doing so; and as it happened, it was
better she should not have made the attempt
that night, for another intrusion, a very different
one from the last, would have obliged her to
get up again.

CHAPTER III.

GOING BEYOND SEAS.

In the middle of the night some one knocked very gently at the door, and when Joan had cautiously opened it, a low but eager voice said:

"Is this Mrs. Coggle's house?"

"Yes; but who may you be?" Joan inquired.

"I am Mrs. Yates, Joan; let me in."

"Mrs. Yates, of all the fishes in the sea! And the baby, too, I do declare. Come in, ma'am, come in;" and taking the infant from its mother's arms, Joan led the way to the parlor.

"Well, mistress, if the Missy as you wanted to see is not come her own self to see you. Here's Mrs. Yates."

"Good gracious, ma'am, you are very welcome. I'm sure it's a mercy that you and your babe are not burnt alive. But where is Mr. Yates?"

"Take the child a moment, mistress," Joan said, "whilst I looks after this poor lady; she is like to faint, I think. Sit down, ma'am. Take that heavy cloak off, and rest your head against the back of the chair, whilst I fetches you a drop of cowslip wine."

The young woman thus addressed was not more than twenty-one or two years of age, very thin and delicate, but singularly lovely. Her large blue eyes were fringed with dark eyelashes, and her hair and eyebrows were black also. The dark shade under those eyes enhanced their beauty, but made the pale face look paler still. She sipped some of the wine Joan held to her lips; then stretched out her arms for her baby, and burst into tears. When it was laid on her knees they fell in torrents on its little form. For some minutes she seemed utterly unable to utter a word.

Mrs. Coggle whispered to Joan, "Do you think her husband is dead?"

Mrs. Yates heard the question, and it roused her from her grief.

"No, no, thank God, he is not dead, and I

ought not to weep so bitterly as God has
spared him to me. But I must make haste to
tell you why I have come here, and what I
want to ask you to do for me. My husband
and myself are going to sail for France this
very night. It is already noised about that
this fire is the work of the Papists, and to-
morrow noted Catholics will be in danger of
their lives. Mr. Grant was arrested an hour
ago, and we have had secret information that a
warrant has been issued for Mr. Yates's appre-
hension. His cousin William has been watching for an opportunity to denounce him as a
lapsed recusant, that he may succeed to his
property, and this panic has doubtless served
his turn. If my husband were to be thrown
into prison he would never survive it. In his
delicate state of health the bad air and close
confinement would kill him. We must, therefore, fly at once. A friend of ours, the captain
of a vessel now at the mouth of the river, will
convey us straight away to France. Mr. Yates
is waiting for me with a boat at the landing-
place near the bridge. I could not let him go

alone, but what can we do with baby? I have no friend in London with whom I can leave her. She is, as you know, scarcely three weeks old, and this is the first time she has been out of the house. We cannot venture to take her with us. The shock I sustained on suddenly opening a letter which informed me of William's design against us drove the milk from my breast. I cannot nurse my child, and there is no time to procure proper food for her; and then the stormy weather and the rough sea.—O my God, my God! It is dreadful whichever way I look at it."

Mrs. Yates pressed her hand on her heart, and then her lips moved in prayer. At the end of a few instants she regained her composure, and said to Mrs. Coggle:

"I thought you would perhaps help me; that you would keep baby till I can come and fetch her."

There was an irresistibly earnest, pleading look in the poor young mother's face as she said this that would have touched a harder heart than the Widow Coggle's.

"Well, ma'am," she answered, "the poor dear lamb is for sure too wee a thing to go a-tossing about the world, not to speak of the sea; and I would on no account say nay to you in your distress, seeing how your worshipful family dealt with my good husband for so many years before you was ever born."

"I know you are fond of children, Mrs. Coggle. I am sure you will take great care of my poor little Mary."

"O yes, madam; you need not fear about that," Mrs. Coggle replied, wiping her eyes. "And though Joan calls babies fudge, she has a good heart at bottom, and will be kind, I am sure, to little Missy. Won't you, Joan?"

This appeal to Joan's feelings was answered with a gruffness that did not alarm Mrs. Yates. In confiding her child to Mrs. Coggle's care, her chief comfort was in the thought of Joan's sterling worth; and the way in which the hard rugged hand of the old servant returned the pressure of her own, which she had held out to her in silence, conveyed more than words would have done.

"Now, as to money," she said, turning to Mrs. Coggle, who was not sorry to hear the subject mentioned, though, to do her justice, she would not at that moment have alluded to it herself; "I will leave with you these twenty pounds, and write to you when I arrive in France to arrange about baby's coming to us as soon as it is safe for her to travel. O my God, will the day ever come? Shall I ever see her again?"

"O yes, ma'am, if it pleases God you will; and you does not want anything but what pleases Him," Joan whispered to the poor mother, who was pressing her child to her heart as if she would never let it go.

"There is a knock at the door," she exclaimed. It must be Mr. Yates's servant come for me. He was to fetch me when all was ready. I must—I must go."

"You must take something first," Mrs. Coggle said. "Let me get you something hot to drink."

Mrs. Yates shook her head, and made a sign that she wanted nothing. Then once more pressing her lips on her baby's little face, she murmured, " My own precious one ; may God's blessed Mother watch over you!" Then, turning to Mrs. Coggle, she said somewhat timidly, "I should have liked to have hung this chain and cross round her neck, but I am afraid of getting you into trouble. But will you put it by for baby, and show it her sometimes when she begins to take notice?"

Mrs. Coggle hesitated, and said that the times were likely to be troublesome, and she did not like to keep ever so small a crucifix in her house. Mrs. Yates sighed, and was hiding the cross in her dress, when Joan whispered to her mistress:

"Look here, ma'am, do you go into the back parlor and fetch out of the cupboard a piece of the seed cake for Mrs. Yates. Here's the keys. If she won't eat it now, she can put it into her pocket against the sea-air makes her hungry." Then, seizing her opportunity, she said, "Give me that cross, Mrs. Yates; I'll take care of it. It won't do no harm to nobody."

"O, but if it were to bring you into trouble."

"Never you be afraid; but look here, I want to know has this here child been baptized?"

"O yes, the very day she was born."

"And by a real downright Catholic priest?"

"Yes, by one of our own good fathers. Joan, if I was to die, and my husband also, you would be sure to see that baby was brought up in our holy faith?"

Joan considered an instant, and then answered: "Well, as to the bringing up of her, that's more than I can promise. You see, ma'am, them as should have their way in this world does not always get it, I'm thinking. But if you don't come back, and this child lives to know black from white, and Joan Porter is alive then, she shall hear from her that you and her father were good Catholics."

Mrs. Yates did not speak, but she placed her baby in Joan's arms, and gave her one of those looks which remain forever in the memory of those who understand their silent eloquence. Mrs. Coggle returned at that moment with a large piece of cake, which she succeeded in thrusting into Mrs. Yates's pocket; and then,

with a desperate effort, the poor young mother
tore herself away, and left the house. How
dark the narrow street looked, how cold the
night air felt, as she followed the steps of the
servant who was guiding her! At each opening toward the river she caught sight of the
fire, and the whole of the sky bore a lurid and
threatening aspect.

CHAPTER IV.

AT the appointed place Mrs. Yates found her husband waiting for her. She whispered to him that Baby was safely housed, and then they stepped into the boat. She did not shed a tear until they had got some way down the river—beyond the crowd of barges, through which the rowers had slowly made their way. But when the burning city had faded from her view; when the air which had seemed loaded with foul vapors began to blow freshly from the green fields, and naught but the red glare still visible in the distance gave evidence of the fearful conflagration, which without that sign would have seemed like a hideous dream; when her husband, weak with illness, and exhausted by the sufferings and emotions of the preceding hours, had at last fallen asleep by her side; when she had time to think and to feel, then her tears began to flow. She thought of the home of her childhood, the old house in Berkshire, embosomed in trees and mirrored in the river; of her mother's grave, and the little domestic chapel, and the library where her aged father was wont to spend his lonely evenings and had blessed her for the last time; of her own house in London, where she had lived since her marriage; of many a little incident of those two happy years; of the joy with which her child had been welcomed into a world of sorrow; of the parting with her, and the utter uncertainty of the future. She looked on the pallid and wan face of her young husband with the presentiment of an impending grief. To look on sleep and think of death! Who has not known the anguish of that silent contemplation? She mused on the happy past, the sad present, and the gloomy future, and could not refrain from weeping.

But sorrows, separations, and bereavements did not take Catholics by surprise in those days. They were their daily bread, their habitual portion. It might be said of them, as of the first Christians, that except for the hope of the resurrection, they were of all men most miserable. Friends, home, fortune, and life itself were held by so frail a tenure that the world to come was the great reality ever present to their mental vision. It is remarkable how much the books of devotion of that period dwell on the anticipations of heaven—what glowing pictures they draw of that excellent land of promise, the haven of security, the place of refuge, the garden of eternal flowers, and the crown of just persons, ever contrasting its imperishable joys with the nothingness of earth. Detachment and resignation were virtues continually needed and at the same time easily practised by those who, if they were true to their faith, were necessarily unworldly; who could not even attempt to serve both God and Mammon. This trained them to an habitual spirit of endurance, a strong-hearted if not light-hearted acceptance of what they were never for an instant secure from—the most sudden reverse of circumstances, the most total overthrow of home ties and domestic happiness.

Mrs. Yates had never reckoned on the con-

tinuance of the peace she had hitherto enjoyed.
The trial that had come upon her had been
anticipated and prepared for on her knees by
daily meditations on the Passion of Christ and
a diligent study of the lives of the early Christians. Amongst the English martyrs who during
the preceding hundred years had sealed with
their blood their fidelity to the Church she
counted relatives whose names were enshrined
as heirlooms in the hearts of many an old
Catholic family with whom her own was connected. This had given her, even as a child, a
nobleness of soul well adapted to meet dangers
and sufferings not only with patience but with
a kind of holy joy. For one moment, indeed,
grief had bowed her down. She thought of the
infant whom she had left sleeping on Joan Porter's knees, and of the distance between them,
which each instant was increasing. She glanced
first at her husband's face, then at the sky and
the bright stars above her head, and at the
dark waters on each side of them, and before
her mind rose a vision of the flight into Egypt,
sad, sudden, and desolate as theirs. "But

Jesus was with them," the mother's heart
whispered.

At that moment she caught the sound of her
beloved one's voice murmuring in its sleep
words he had been constantly in the habit of
repeating during his long illness, " Jesu, Deus
meus, super omnia amo te." They seemed to
answer her unspoken thought. She turned to
Him who was with them in that lonely hour as
He was with Mary and Joseph in the pathless
desert, and she found rest to her soul. All was
committed to Him—all left in His hands—and
when the faint light of dawning day broke in
the east, and the sea was in sight with its rough
waves and foaming breakers, she looked upon
it without shrinking, and said in her heart,
" Magnificat anima mea Dominum, et exaltavit
spiritus meus in Deo salutari meo."

CHAPTER V.

IT NEVER RAINS BUT IT POURS.

WHILE Mrs. Yates and her husband were gliding down the river in the dark hours of the night, and the conflagration was continuing to rage in the doomed city, Mrs. Coggle and Joan Porter were anxiously engaged in ministering to the comfort of the little creature that had been left in their charge. After feeding it with the bottle, Joan had consigned it to the immediate care of her mistress whilst she unpacked the bundle of clothes which Mrs. Yates had brought with her. The baby apparently resented being thus transferred, and began to exert that wonderful power of lungs which those unacquainted with the strength of infants in this respect would never suppose such small beings possessed of. Mrs. Coggle was quite distressed at the way in which little Missy screamed.

" Joan, what shall I do?" she exclaimed.

" Sing," was the laconic answer she received.

" It is easy to say sing, but what shall I sing? The Hundredth Psalm?"

" The Hundredth Psalm!   Now, ma'am, whatever you do, don't go for to sing to that child those croaking tunes which you hears, the more shame for you, begging your pardon, at the Protestant church.   Do you think they'll put a Catholic baby to sleep, bless it? Can't you sing ' Margery Daw'?"

Thus directed, Mrs. Coggle intoned,

> "See saw, Margery Daw
> Sold her bed and laid on straw."

And, strange to say, in spite of the shrill, cracked voice with which the ditty was sung, it seemed to possess a soporific power.   Either the charm of music or the rocking motion which accompanied it produced the desired effect, and Missy soon fell asleep.   Whilst she slumbered the following colloquy took place between Mrs. Coggle and Joan.

" What a lot of nice clothes those are!" the

former observed. "They will last the little miss a long time."

"Yes, they be something like what a child like that should have. Is she asleep?"

"Yes; fast, I do declare."

"Mrs. Yates said she had been feeding her by hand for a fortnight past. She takes to the bottle beautiful."

"Well, if the world is not full of troubles, Joan."

"I think, ma'am, it's like cats, the older it grows the worser it be."

"After all, it ain't such a bad world to everybody; I knows of some in it who have nothing to complain of!"

"Lord bless you, ma'am! it would be a very good world if He as made it had His own way in it, and folks would only do as He bids them. I'm speaking of what people makes it by their wickedness."

"I'm a-thinking of the ladies I used to see at my late mistress's. They must be as happy as the day is long in their fine houses and with their coaches and four, and then such a lot o' dresses! I do declare some of them had a new one every month in the year!"

"Well, to my mind, that's a queer sort of a happiness. The bother it must be to have to order one's coach each time one has a mind to go abroad, and to eat one's victuals as fine folks do, with half-a-dozen men staring at them all the time; and as to the gowns!—but laws me, talking of gowns, I'll tell you what, ma'am, you'd better give me that ere baby; she'll be the better for being undressed and put into one of these here nightgowns, and tucked into my bed between two pillows, as we ain't got a cradle for her; and will you mean time fill again this bottle with warm milk and water, and bring it upstairs with you?"

The baby was carried off by Joan with a clumsy tenderness, and Mrs. Coggle set about obeying her commands. While occupied in this way, various highly philosophical though somewhat desultory reflections were passing through her mind, such as "Dear me, we never know what a day may bring forth! to think of me talking of Mrs. Biddle's suppers, and then this fire to happen! What a shocking thing a fire is! nobody knows where it begins or where it will end. I wonder how far twenty pounds will serve for to bring up a child; it is for certain a great deal of money, but the heaviest purse grows light at last. It is not easy to come back from beyond seas, or to send money from so far. Well, I may as well take up those gold pieces Mrs. Yates has left on the table, before I carry up this bottle."

Just as this had been accomplished, and Mrs. Coggle was leaving the room, the sound of a voice and a knock at the door once more arrested her ascent, and threw her, as she expressed it, all in a tremble again. The knocking was hurriedly repeated; and she cried out,

"Who's there?"

The voice answered,

"A neighbor; quick, quick; open the door."

Mrs. Coggle withdrew the bolts, exclaiming in a fretful manner,

"I wish, whosoever you be, that you would not flurry folks this way;" and then, in a

louder voice, "Mrs. Peterkin, I declare.
God bless my soul! what brings you here
again?"

The individual thus addressed advanced into
the room, holding something in her arms, wrapt
up in a blue shawl; before she could speak, a
sound of crying proceeded from the bundle,
and, to Mrs. Coggle's amazement, another
infant met her eyes.

"Look here, ma'am," Mrs. Peterkin said;
"I've brought you this baby."

"Lord bless you, Mrs. Peterkin, we've got
one already. We don't want another, I promise
you," the widow replied in a tone of despair.

"O, but whatever you do, ma'am, you must
take this one in for the night."

"And, in the name of goodness, whose is it,
and where does it come from?"

"From t'other side of the river; that's all I
know for the present," Mrs. Peterkin replied.
"My John was standing opposite to a large
house, a-looking at it burning—he is always a-
standing a-looking at something—when a man
comes to the window with a child in his arms,

and cries to John, 'Hold out your hands and catch hold of this infant. There's nothing but flames behind me.' No sooner said than done, and the babe dropt into his arms. Like a fool, he runs away with it till he meets me. 'There,' says he, 'I'm rid of it,' and pops it into my hands with nothing but this shawl on; and before I can turn round he is off again like a shot to the fire. Now, Mrs. Coggle, you was once used to babies, and I never was. If you are a Christian woman, you'll take charge of this one to-night, and to-morrow I'll warrant you its friends will come for it, and offer you something handsome for your trouble."

"But if it has no friends, and nobody comes?" Mrs. Coggle rejoined, with justifiable misgivings.

Mrs. Peterkin assured her that as the child had tumbled out of a big house it certainly must have rich friends, and said that if the worst came to the worst it could go to the workhouse or the foundling hospital, and then declared that she could not stay any longer, and, suiting the action to her words, deposited the child on a chair, and took to her heels, crying out as she ran away,

"Good-night to ye, Mrs. Coggle; good- . night, and many thanks to ye for taking charge of the babe."

Poor Mrs. Coggle stood petrified for a moment, and then began screaming,

"I say, Mrs. Peterkin; I say, ma'am, will you stop? You are a neat article for to go and leave this here child on my chairs and in my hands. Whatever will Joan say? O my goodness, it's beginning to cry! Joan, Joan; for pity's sake come here!"

A voice cried from the top of the stairs,

"Gracious me, mistress, will you bring the bottle? Do you want for to starve this infant?"

"Starve it!" Mrs. Coggle retorted, in an indignant manner; "one bottle won't do for two; and goodness knows how we shall manage. Here's another child saved from the fire."

"Lord save us!" Joan exclaimed. "It never rains but it pours babies anyways. And, in the name of patience, how did it come here, mistress?"

"The widow Peterkin, of course, she brought it in," Mrs. Coggle replied ; and began pouring forth her indignant feelings.

But Joan was not listening. Her attention was taken up by the child, whose little hands and feet she was chafing.

"Why, it's just as cold as a stone all over," she cried. "One would have thought the fire might have done so much as to warm it."

And against her bosom she warmed the little creature, and then carried it into her room up-stairs, and put on it one of the night-gowns of Mrs. Yates's baby, and laid it by the side of the first comer in the bed between two pillows, and fed each alternately from the same bottle till the two little children, looking like birds in a nest, fell asleep side by side. All the remainder of the night these good women hovered round that bed. When one of the babies screamed it was taken up, fed, dandled, and walked about the room, or else rocked on the knees of one or the other of its nurses.

Toward morning the whole party dozed off When Mrs. Coggle opened her eyes the light was streaming into the room. She rubbed her eyes, and asked,

"Has it been all a dream, Joan, about the fire and the babies?"

"No, mistress. It isn't a dream at all, by the same token that here they are as large, or I suppose I should say, as small, as life. There's Mrs. Yates's missy, a sucking of its thumb as if she had the use of reason."

"What are you talking about, Joan?" Mrs. Coggle said, taking up the other child. "This is Mrs. Yates's baby."

"No more than she's mine, ma'am."

"Dear me, Joan; I'm likely to know better than you. I'll forswear myself this one was lying nearest the wall."

"Don't forswear yourself, mistress. That was the first time you took her up for to feed her. Lord bless you! they changed places this blessed night as often as in a country dance. But I knows very well which is which."

"That's more than I do. I wish we had tied a thread round their arms for to make sure."

"Good gracious, ma'am, what a fidget you

are. This here child is Mrs. Yates's; and that's the babe what Mrs. Peterkin brought you."

The sound of that lady's name reawakened Mrs. Coggle's ire.

" Do you think she will soon come to let us know what to do with it ? "

" She come ! Yes, if the parents have turned up, and there's something to be got by it."

" But, then, what shall we do, Joan ? "

" The best we can, ma'am," was Joan's laconic reply.

Then, as both babies began to squall, the conversation ended for the time being, but the dispute began that morning was destined to be often renewed.

CHAPTER VI.

AN EVENTFUL DAY.

NEARLY three years had elapsed since the events detailed in the last chapter, and during all that time the little house near Westminster bridge had known no change. Mrs. Coggle and Joan Porter had not been relieved of either of their charges. Mrs. Peterkin had not returned and Mrs. Yates had not written. Rumors had reached London that the vessel in which she had sailed had been shipwrecked on the coast of France. Joan was inclined to think that this must have been the case, for Mrs. Yates would never have been so long without communication with them had she still been in existence. Her love for the little Mary increased in proportion to what she believed to be her orphaned condition. She was fond of both the children so strangely left on their hands in the same night; but Mrs. Yates's

Polly was much nearer to her heart than the one Mrs. Peterkin had consigned to Mrs. Coggle's reluctant arms. The latter, however, had taken a decided fancy to the child they knew nothing about, and indulged in romantic expectations as to her future fate. Joan perceived clearly that her mistress had no distinct impressions as to the identity of the children, but would seize upon whatever opportunity offered of settling the matter according to her desires. Her own conviction was positive. It was an actual certainty, and she succeeded so far in establishing the fact that Polly was Polly Yates, that neither Mrs. Coggle nor any one else called her by any other name; and the other child, who had been conditionally baptized by Joan's strenuous exertions, and named Sarah, was never spoken of but as Sally. Still a feeble protest against this decision was occasionally uttered by the widow, and the dispute, though held in abeyance, was capable of being resumed at any moment. Meantime Sally was her decided favorite, whilst Polly was Joan's darling. She

used to talk to her for hours together of her
mother, and often showed her the little crucifix which at other times she kept carefully
locked up in the drawer. The clothes Mrs.
Yates had left served for both children till
they had outgrown them. Since then their
place had been supplied by Joan's unwearied
industry and generosity. She had secretly
sold, one after another, some valuable trinkets
which had been given her as tokens of gratitude and regard by various persons whom she
had obliged in days of trial and persecution.
Her mother had been a servant in the household of the Spanish ambassador, Don Pedro de
Zuniga; and when a little girl she had lived in
Spitalfields, in the house of Doña Luisa de Carvajal, a saintly lady of that nation, who had for-
saken her country and all her worldly posses-
sions in order to devote herself to a life of
poverty and labor in London, with the sole
object of encouraging, assisting, and instructing
the suffering Catholics of every rank in that city.
Her house was in reality a convent, established
in the very centre of raging heresy and in the

face of dire persecution. Joan had been employed by her as a little messenger of mercy on many and many an occasion, and had learned lessons under that roof which she had never forgotten. Throughout her life she had practised them, and carried consolation to many a breaking heart, and even saved several lives through her intelligent exertions, discreet prudence, and boundless courage. When she receceived any gifts from rich persons, they were set aside for the poor; and thus she was enabled to assist her mistress in supporting the little children thrown on their hands.

Three years, as we have said, elapsed tranquilly without any event to mark them; but there came a day which made a great change in that peaceful household. One of the children, little Sally, was seized one morning with violent convulsions; the doctor was sent for, and prescribed, but without any good results. Vain were Mrs. Coggle's tears, vain poor Joan's prayers, that if it pleased God that little life should be spared; for though she did not love Sally as much as Polly, her heart ached sorely when she saw death in the face of the fair little creature lying on her knees, and felt it was all over. She breathed her last about six o'clock in the evening; and Joan carried the small corpse to the bed where, since the night of the fire, the two children had always slept together, and the following words fell from her lips as she laid it out:

"Good-by, dear little one. We sha'n't never know your real name, and there will be nobody but me to remember you and think as how you have been a sister to Polly. You are gone, poor lamb, to a better world than this; and them as were your parents on earth may be looking out for you there; but, anyways, there is one that loves you more than they did, who is a welcoming of you."

On the day of the funeral, which Mrs. Coggle had not courage to attend, she sat at home with Polly on her knees, and felt so disconsolate that a visit even from Mrs. Crump proved a relief. After a few words of inquiry as to the illness and death of the other child, and friendly notice of the surviving one, Mrs. Crump said she hoped this little missy would not die too.

"Die! Lord bless you!" Mrs. Coggle replied, 'she's not a thinking on it. She sleeps like a top and eats like a Turk. Dear, dear, it's very hard to have to bury one child, and to support another, and all the time not to know which is dead and which is alive."

"What do you mean, Mrs. Coggle? This one is alive, and t'other's dead. What's the bother?"

"Why, you see, ma'am, the bother is this. Joan has always had it that this is Mrs. Yates's child, but I say she is the one as Mrs. Peterkin brought from the fire. We were fools that night not to tie a bit of tape or something on their arms by which we might know them from each other. But we put them to sleep in the same bed, and our heads were confused, I take it, and they had on the same nightgowns what belonged to Mrs. Yates; and one of us fed the one and then the other, and never thought much till the morning which was which. Then, when it came to distinguishing them, says Joan,

'This is Polly Yates.' 'No,' says I, 'this is she;' and so we goes on, No, no, Yes, yes, like Punch and Judy, and never could agree. But Joan had the last word—she is a terrible one for that, and has always called this child Polly."

The sound of her name caught the attention of the little girl, and she began to sing, " Polly, put the kettle on."

" Joan taught her to sing that on purpose, I think," Mrs. Coggle exclaimed. " Where we shall get money to feed this child, God only knows. Mr. and Mrs. Yates have been drowned, I take it, long ago, and we shall get nothing from them. All is so dear now, and folks get old. I'm sure I wonder how ever Joan can work as she does."

Mrs. Crump thought some folk lived on work and some died of it, which struck Mrs. Coggle as a very sensible remark. She should certainly die if she worked half as hard as Joan.

" If I was you," Mrs. Crump went on to say, " I would not give in about that child. I've an idea that if you stick to your notion about her, she will turn out to be the daughter of some grand folks or other, and be the making of you."

"You're just saying what I keep saying to Joan. I'm always expecting something to happen. And every day when I awake, I says to myself, 'Now this may be the day on which something will happen.'

If any one perseveres in this practice the prevision must at last be realized; and it so happened that that very day and hour something did happen which considerably changed the face of affairs in the house by the bridge side.

Mrs. Crump was beginning one of her long stories about the way in which she and Mrs. Peterkin had quarrelled and parted company before the latter had left London to go and live with her aunt at Dover, from whom she had expectations, when a little maid-of-all-work, who had been recently added to Mrs. Coggle's establishment, came in and said that there was a lady at the door in a chair asking to see her mistress.

Mrs. Coggle felt her heart beating very fast. No lady had been to see her for a long time.

She glanced at the glass to see her cap was straight, and hastily took off her apron.

"Ask the lady to walk in," she said, in an agitated voice. She would have liked to request Mrs. Crump to walk out. A bright idea struck her. "Now, will you do me a favor?" she said; "just take this child upstairs and wash her face and hands, and put on her new kirtle and her white cap, in case the lady, whoever she be, asks to see her."

There was some chance that Polly would set up a roar on being led out of the room by Mrs. Crump; but an assurance that there was a piece of sugar in that lady's pocket, which she should have if she were good, checked the outburst, and Mrs. Coggle was left alone to receive her visitor.

A tall, pretty, and very smartly-dressed person came into the room, and, in a manner which betrayed not much emotion, but some agitation, said,

"I suppose you do not remember me, Mistress Coggle. I am Lady Davenant."

"I beg your ladyship's pardon. I did not

recollect you at first ; but now I do. I am not like to forget Mrs. Mordaunt's daughter."

" Yes, I know you were very much attached to my mother. I suppose you heard, at the time, of the death of my husband and my child ? "

" I heard speak of Sir William's death, my lady, but I did not know that your ladyship had any children. Since Mrs. Mordaunt died, I seldom had news of the family."

" About six weeks before the fire of London, I had been confined of a little girl ; it was in trying to save her that my husband was burnt to death. I lost them both that dreadful night."

" Dear me, my lady, what a mercy you did not die too ! It was a cruel night for many poor souls. I'm sure Joan and I, we'll never forget it. And did you go abroad then ? "

" Yes ; my uncle Mordaunt carried me with him to the south of France, and I have lived with him ever since. He is a great invalid, and cannot bear me to leave him. I was obliged, however, to come to England on some business of his, and I thought I would call and see you."

" I am sure it is very kind of you, my lady.

It is not often as I have the pleasure of a visit
from the likes of you."

At that moment a sudden thumping at the
door made Lady Davenant start; she seemed
very nervous, and when the thumps were
seconded by a childish voice calling out, " Open,
Coggy—go 'way, Missy Cump! go 'way!" her
color changed.

"Have you a child living with you?" she
asked. "Is it a girl? let her come in." The
door was opened, and like a living picture of
childlike beauty, Polly stood before her, half-
triumphant at having got into the room, half-
abashed at the sight of a stranger, covering her
eyes with her little hand, and peeping through
her fingers at the dazzling appearance of the
lady in her flowered dress, high heels, and flow-
ing curls.

"What a pretty child!" Lady Davenant exclaimed. "Come here, my sweet one; come
and speak to me."

Polly hesitated; but the sight of a gold
locket held out by the stranger induced her
to come forward, and she consented to stand

by her side and to examine her various trinkets.

Lady Davenant stroked her cheek, patted her head, kissed her forehead, and at last said to her, "What is your name, sweet little puss?"

"She does not know it, my lady; she does not know who she is," Mrs. Coggle quickly replied.

But Polly, to disprove that assertion, cried out immediately, "Me's Polly."

"You call her Polly, I suppose, but do you know who she is?"

"Not in the least, my lady."

The color rose in Lady Davenant's cheeks, and she said, "Tell me all you know about her."

"Nothing, my lady, except that one Mrs. Peterkin brought her here the night of the fire, three years ago."

"That she did," said Mrs. Crump, who had followed Polly into the room. "It's as true as I'm alive; I met her carrying the child in her arms."

" And she left her on that chair—that one on which you are sitting, my lady—and never has been heard of since."

" I have heard from her, and I have seen her, at Dover," Lady Davenant exclaimed. " She found out my direction, and wrote to me to Montpellier to say that a child had been thrown out of the window of a house, which she had since by accident learned was Sir William Davenant's, and that her friend Mrs. Coggle—"

" Friend! good gracious! the impudence of the woman!"

" Well, she said you had taken charge of the child, and that she did not doubt that the little girl she left with you was mine. I spoke to her on my way at Dover, and she adhered to her story. Now tell me, what do you think? Is there anything that could help to prove it?"

" I'm thinking—O yes, of course, the shawl. Wait a moment, I'll get it."

Lady Davenant sat gazing at Polly, quite satisfied that she was one of the prettiest children she had ever seen. " She does not look like a lowborn, common child," she ejaculated, as she stroked the soft silken hair that curled round Polly's little face.

" No, to be sure not, my lady, nor never did from the first day she came to this roof. She was always the genteelest little creature, the delicatest infant."

" O, heavens ! " Lady Davenant exclaimed, as Mrs. Coggle returned with the blue shawl in her hands. " There can be no doubt about it— not a shadow of a doubt. That is my shawl, by the same token that my good mother gave it me as part of my wedding gear. Look here ! There is a bit of the fringe missing. I perfectly remember, the day before the fire, as I was passing through a narrow passage a nail caught and tore it off. You swear that this child was wrapped in that shawl on the night she was brought to you?"

" My lady, I do most solemnly swear that the child that Mrs. Peterkin brought to this house on the night of the Fire of London was wrapped up in that shawl."

" That's enough, quite enough for me; your testimony, and Mrs. Peterkin's, and this good

woman's," she added, turning to Mrs. Crump,
"all bear evidence to what my heart wishes to
believe and tells me is true."

As she said these words, Lady Davenant lifted
up Polly to her knees, and pressing her to her
heart said, "My own little darling, I am your
mother."

"Where's oo coss?" Polly asked.

"What—what does she say?"

"I want oo coss."

"O, nonsense, Polly, nonsense, look at the
lady's beautiful rings. My lady, I do feel certain
this is your child, and I have always said so."

"That she has, through thick and thin, my
lady," Mrs. Crump testified, who had often been
present at the disputes on that point.

"I am overjoyed, Mrs. Coggle, at finding my
little Rose. Rose is her name, and you must
not call her Polly any more. How good it is
of you to have taken care of her so long and
dressed her so nicely, and without any remu-
neration! But now I shall pay, if you please, a
regular pension for her. I wish to leave Rose
with you for the present; I must return im-

mediately to Montpellier. Mr. Mordaunt expects me back before the end of the month, and I must not disappoint him. He is an old man now, and I am bound to attend to all his wishes. He cannot endure children, and I am afraid it will be difficult to make him understand or believe that Rose is alive. I am sure he will say there is not sufficient proof of it. Let me see, there is Mrs. Peterkin's assertion that this dear child was thrown out of a window at Davenant House; I asked her if her son would confirm her statement, but he is dead, it seems; and then this shawl—I am sure that I cannot be mistaken about it; this fact of the rent in it, you see, is conclusive. Did Mrs. Peterkin tell you it was out of Davenant House that the child was thrown?"

"No, my lady; I can't remember that she did. She said it was a large house on the other side of the river."

"Exactly; and that tallying with the production of this shawl, I am perfectly satisfied. But if you knew Mr. Mordaunt! He always takes the opposite view to that of other people; and when he has once pronounced an opinion, he will not endure to be contradicted."

"That is just like Joan Porter. It's no use to withstand her when she has made up her mind upon anything," Mrs. Coggle observed, with a sigh.

"My uncle quarrelled with his sister's son, Mr. George Yates, because he married against his advice; and nothing could induce him to forgive them. He will probably leave me his fortune, who am his niece only by marriage; but I am obliged to take the greatest care not to offend him. He is so strangely suspicious, too. He always thinks people are trying to deceive him. I once said, 'How strange it would be if by some possibility my little baby had been saved, and I should find out that, after all, she was alive!' He went quite into a passion, and said scornfully, 'Your ladyship'—he always addresses me in that way when he is angry—'your ladyship had better express that hope publicly, and plenty of knaves and impostors will produce beggars' brats to palm them upon you!'"

"O good gracious!" Mrs. Crump exclaimed,

"to think of Mrs. Coggle being called such names!"

"Indeed, I never meant to speak of *her* as such. Please do not cry, my good Mrs. Coggle. I might not have relied wholly on Mrs. Peterkin's statement, but I believe every word you say. And then, you know, I can swear to this shawl, that it was mine. Perhaps in time, and with great prudence, I may be able to bring Mr. Mordaunt to admit that this is my little Rose. In any case, when it shall please God to remove him from this world, I can then openly adopt her. In the meantime how very fortunate it is that she should have fallen into your hands : you, who lived with my poor mother so many years that I quite look upon you as a friend."

"I am sure your ladyship is very good to say so," Mrs. Coggle said with a sigh, and glancing uneasily at the door, having heard a sound resembling some one opening the one on the street. Feeling desperate, she whispered to Mrs. Crump, "For pity's sake, go and see who's in the passage, and if it's Joan don't let her come in."

Lady Davenant kissed and fondled the child on her knees, and then went on saying, " It was very good of you to take such care of Rose, when you did not know who she was, and no one paid for her support. I am obliged to leave London directly. Mr. Mordaunt cannot possibly spare me any longer, and my future prospects depend entirely upon him. I shall write and tell you all my wishes about this dear little new-found girl of mine."

" I shall be sure to attend to them, my lady."

" Here are fifty pounds to begin with," Lady Davenant said. "I brought this sum with me in case I should find Mrs. Peterkin's statement confirmed. I would like you to hire at once a nice cottage at Spitalfields, or Islington, or Paddington—somewhere out of town, where there would be a garden, and Rose could run about on the grass. She is really a very pretty child. You must get her everything she ought to have in the way of dress—everything my child ought to wear. Some nice kirtles and embroidered kerchiefs and smart lace caps with ribbons. And take particular care of her hair

and complexion; do not let her go out in the
sun without a veil.   Write to me often how
she is.   By the way, here is my direction, 16
Grande Rue, Montpellier, France.   I have
written it on this card."

Mrs. Coggle courtesied, and longed for Lady
Davenant to be out of the house.   Time to
persuade and manage Joan Porter, two objects
difficult of attainment as she had herself just
stated, were important at that moment, and she
counted the minutes whilst Lady Davenant
caressed the little girl and renewed her thanks
for past care and directions for the future.   At
last she opened the door and took her departure, Mrs. Crump accompanying her to her
chair, and then withdrawing herself, with a
prudent wish not to be present at the conversation likely to ensue between Joan Porter and
her mistress.

The latter sat in a very confused state of
mind, dancing the child on her knee and singing in a nervously cheerful manner, " Polly,
put the kettle on ; " and then, alarmed at having said Polly, turned it to " Rosy, put the
3

kettle on," which drew a remonstrance from Polly. " Polly, not Rosy," she said, with the dislike children always feel at a change in what they have been accustomed to. " Oo must say Polly. Rosy not put the kettle on."

" O, well, never mind, my dear. It's all the same thing. Take your doll now, and go and play by yourself."

Polly having graciously consented to this, poor Mrs. Coggle sat with her eyes fixed on the fire, with the following thoughts passing through her mind. " What *will* Joan say? She has no business to say anything. She is only my servant. I always maintained Polly was not Polly. I am sure in any case she had better have a living mother, and one that can provide for her, and a cottage in the country, and nice clothes and all. I always said she was born with a silver spoon in her mouth, and it would turn up at last; and so it has. But what will Joan say? I don't care. There, I declare I think she's coming! I am all in a tremble.. What a silly creature I am! She is only my servant."

CHAPTER VII.

JOAN'S RESOLUTION.

WHEN Joan returned from the funeral of the poor little nameless Sally, as she had always called her, she found her mistress sitting over the fire in a musing attitude, which she took for one of deep melancholy, and she proceeded accordingly to administer consolation in the following manner:

"Cheer up, ma'am. Everything is best as it is. Thank God, the poor little soul has been baptized, conditional or not conditional, and has gone straight to heaven, like an arrow from a bow. So don't you look sad. One child is enough for old folks like us to bring up. Polly here will give us enough to care for for many a long year."

Mrs. Coggle felt it necessary at that moment to strike a decisive blow, and, summoning up her courage, said, "Joan, it's no use for to go on calling that child Polly; she ain't Polly at all: and now from this day you must call her Rose—for that's her name as much as yours is Joan—and moreover she is Miss Rose Davenant. It is all found out. Her mother has been here."

"Is it Mrs. Yates you mean?" Joan added, bewildered by this assertion.

"No; Lady Davenant. She has heard from Mrs. Peterkin the short and the long of the story, by letter and by mouth."

"That last, I take it, will have been the long of it," Joan exclaimed. "And what was it she heard, ma'am?"

"That the child was here which had fallen out of the window at Davenant House on the night of the fire, and her ladyship knew her again directly, and the blue shawl too."

"Heaven forgive you, ma'am, that is if you knows what you're about, which I question. Have you really gone for to persuade that poor lady that this child is hers?"

"It needed no persuasion at all. She was as sure of it from the first as that you are standing there."

"Good gracious! but did you tell her Mrs. Yates had left her child here the same night, and that we mixed them up together in her baby's clothes?"

"No, Joan; the least said the soonest mended," Mrs. Coggle replied in an oracular manner.

"Not always, ma'am; there's many a lie as has been said by holding one's tongue," Joan exclaimed indignantly.

"The very minute she saw the shawl she knew it," Mrs. Coggle repeated, with that strange obliquity of mind which belongs to those whose wishes are on one side of a question, and whose reasoning powers are too weak to see the fallacy of their own arguments.

"Well, ma'am, and let her have the shawl, and welcome to it, too. It wrapped up the poor dear child we buried this morning, and if it's a comfort to her to go and see its grave she can do so; but Mrs. Yates's Polly and mine she shall never have, if I can help it."

"Mrs. Yates is dead, Joan; there's no use in harping on what's past."

"I don't know that she *is* dead," Joan retorted;" but if she should be dead five times
over, 'tis no reason to give her child to folks as
won't bring her up in her own faith; why,
them Davenants ain't Catholics at all."

"Now, Joan, for pity's sake don't you talk
aloud of such like-things. The neighbors may
hear you," Mrs. Coggle said, lowering her
voice to a whisper. "It is right against the
law; you'll be the death of us some day.
Those Spanishers you are always telling of
turned your brain about religion."

"God help you, ma'am; if you be speaking
of my sainted mistress, Lady Luisa, I would
have you mind what you say, for I do believe
she is now an angel in heaven, and very like
one she was on earth too. That was why they
was so enraged at her. She gave heart to the
most trembling wretch in fear of torments, when
she spoke of the glory and joy of dying for
Christ."

"Lord save us, how you talk, Joan; it's
enough to make one's hair stand on end. I'm
sure I have enough to think of without your

putting such dismal thoughts in my head. Do you see that power of money in that bag? Do you know how much there's in it? It is Lady Davenant left it here. She wishes me to hire a cottage in the country, and to buy ever so many things for this here little lady. I am sure a better mother never lived. I'm going to consult Mrs. Crump, who has a cousin that lets houses."

Joan made no reply; and her mistress, after fidgeting about the room awhile, counting ostentatiously the gold pieces in the bag, and then locking it up in a drawer, put on her cloak and hood and went out.

Joan sat down and called Polly to her, who jumped on her knees and threw her arms round her neck.

" Where mother's coss?" she asked; "lady got no coss."

Joan's heart was full; she loved this little child with a deep, strong, faithful love, and the thought that she might be robbed of her birthright, that her Polly might be one day severed from the true Church, struck like a dagger into her heart. She silently gave the little crucifix into her tiny hands, and saw her press it to her lips as she had taught her to do.

"Good Jesus—me love Him," little Polly said, and then, slipping off Joan's knees, went back to her playthings.

Joan took up her sewing, and as she watched the little girl running up and down the room, and then stopping short and turning upon her her large, dark blue eyes, full of tenderness and glee—eyes that were unlike any she had ever seen save those of poor Mrs. Yates—she thus soliloquized in a low voice:

"For any one to tell me you are not Polly Yates! when you are as like to your mother as a lamb is to a sheep. Mistress may do as she pleases; get a cottage and buy you finery too, if she likes, with that rich lady's money. She may call you Rose, but for all that you will never be anything but Polly to me, and as long as I live you shall hear from old Joan of your true mother and your Catholic baptism. With my last dying breath I shall witness, my sweet one, that you are her child, and no one else's.

CHAPTER VIII.

SEVERAL months elapsed, and Mrs. Coggle, Joan Porter, and the little girl under their care, had removed from London to a pretty little house in the village of Paddington. Joan had left directions with the neighbors that if any one inquired for her or her mistress, they should be told of their present abode and directed to it. It was more than three years since the night of the fire; from that moment nothing had been seen or heard of Mr. or Mrs. Yates, and all hopes of their return grew more and more faint. On the other hand, regular remittances of money and a variety of presents were made by Lady Davenant to the widow and her little household. Joan had to sustain an unequal combat; her arguments in favor of Mrs. Yates's claims to the child were feeble in comparison with the powerful influence constantly at work on Mrs. Coggle's unreasoning mind. The little girl grew accustomed to hear herself called by two different names, and answered to both.

One day Joan went into London for the purpose of finding out, at the house and street where they used to live, if anything had been heard of a lady returning from foreign parts. She had sometimes been on the same errand before, but never with any success. However, this day the woman who lived next door to her old abode said, that some weeks before, a person dressed in black had called and inquired what was Mrs. Coggle's address. She was pale and sickly-looking, she said, and dressed somewhat shabbily.

"And you gave her our direction?" Joan anxiously asked.

"Well, ma'am, to say the truth, I did not remember it, and could not for the life of me lay my hands on the bit of paper on which you had written it. I asked the lady if I should send it to her, but she said no, she should call again. Howsoever, she has never come back."

"Was she tall," Joan asked, "and had she dark blue eyes?"

"Middle-sized, I should say," was the answer; "and she kept her veil down, so that I did not see her eyes. If you'll write down on that slate near the chimney where you lives, ma'am, I sha'n't lose it as I did the paper."

The mention of this stranger's visit sadly tantalized poor Joan. She resumed her inquiries amongst the Catholics of her acquaintance, but heard no positive tidings of Mrs. Yates. Some said she was dead, others that she had entered a nunnery beyond seas; no one had seen her in London. Some weeks later Joan went to Mass on the Feast of the Assumption, at the Spanish ambassador's chapel, which she had continued now and then to frequent since the days of her childhood, when she had often accompanied there Doña Luisa de Carvajal, and on one occasion been present at a ceremony which had left the deepest impression on her mind. One night her mistress had taken her as usual to the embassy; it was dark when they had arrived there, and Doña Luisa and some of her compan-

ions repaired to the chapel, and spent the evening hours in arranging and adorning it with the
greatest care. An abundance of candles were
placed on the altar ready to be lighted. Beautiful flowers, which they had brought with them,
hung in garlands round the walls, and jewels
and gold ornaments, lent for the purpose by
the ladies of the foreign embassies, adorned the
little sanctuary. Joan's childish admiration
and delight were unbounded. She gave all the
little help in her power to the work that was
going on, and wondered what was the occasion
all this display of grandeur. Vague thoughts
floated in her mind that the king of Spain was
perhaps coming to London, as she had heard
her parents say he did a hundred years ago,
when the queen of England was Catholic. At
last all was finished, and the ladies prayed in
silence before the tabernacle, and Pedro de
Zuniga, the pious ambassador of the Catholic
king, was also on his knees on his fine prie-dieu,
pouring forth fervent supplications, and often
making the sign of the cross on his breast.

Meanwhile the little girl fell fast asleep, and

had confused dreams, in which were blended the Passion of our Lord and visions of heaven, derived from the pictures which she had been gazing on before her eyes had closed. She was wakened from her slumber by the sound of a door opening, and heavy shuffling steps along the passage which led to the chapel, as if men were carrying a heavy weight. The altar had become one blaze of dazzling light, and a mournful strain, faintly played on a musical instrument, accompanied the steps that were approaching. She started to her feet, and saw Doña Luisa standing before her, with a smile of strange beauty on her wan and pallid face.

" Wake up, little one," she said, " wake up, and strew these flowers on the ground where the remains of Christ's martyrs are about to pass."

Roses and lilies, and every kind of bright flowers, were in the basket placed in the child's hands, and she scattered them in hushed silence on the floor of the chapel; whilst the Spanish cavaliers, the young noblemen attached to the embassy, headed by the brave Don Alonzo de Velasco, bore along in triumph the quartered

remains of William Scott and Richard New-
port, two devoted servants of God, who had
died for their faith, and been buried in the
charnel-house of Tyburn. It had been a work
of no ordinary zeal, for the bigoted executioners
had thrust the sacred relics of the martyrs deep
down into the pit, beneath the bodies of assas-
sins and thieves, in the hope that they would
be forever confounded with them. But faith
and love are stronger than hatred and death.
Fired by the burning words of their saintly
countrywoman, the daughter of the house of
Carvajal y Mendoza, the Castilian youths did
not shrink from the loathsome but glorious task.
They sallied forth, twelve of them, in the dead
of night. They feared not to bring those un-
handsome corpses "betwixt the wind and their
nobility" in order to arrive at the treasure they
sought; and when they laid the precious relics
at the foot of the altar, and in the silence of the
night sang the "Te Deum," they had their
meed.

Joan Porter never forgot in after-life that
midnight ceremony, that solemn procession, or

the ethereal light in Doña Luisa's angelic face, as she knelt and kissed the hem of the blood-stained pall which covered the remains of those English martyrs. She never entered that chapel, to which she ever had free access, without that scene rising before her mind, without a prayer that she too might suffer for Christ's sake; and from the well-known picture of the crucifixion over the altar she learnt many a lesson of courage and endurance, which had helped her to meet peril without flinching, and look death in the face, in the service of others.

On the day previously mentioned, at a distance of more than fifty years, she had dwelt as usual on those holy reminiscences, when, lifting up her head, which long had been bowed down in prayer, she caught sight of a woman dressed in black, kneeling at a short distance from her. There came, as she expressed it herself, a lump in her throat and a quick beating at her heart, for something in the figure, and as much of the face as she could see, reminded her strongly of Mrs. Yates. Mass was about to begin. The chapels of the embassies were the only ones at that time where the faithful of London could hear it with a quiet heart. Everywhere else— though year after year, perhaps, the performance of the Holy Sacrifice had escaped notice— a day might come when the ruthless pursuivants would break in, seize the priests, and sometimes scatter the congregation and lay violent hands on the sacred vessels. It was therefore no ordinary privilege to be admitted within the houses where the rights of foreign powers forbade such invasions, and where—thanks to the unwearied prayers and efforts of Doña Luisa de Carvajal— about half a century before, the blessed sacrament was reserved and adored in secret. Joan Porter prayed with her usual fervor—more fervently indeed than ever, but at the same time her eyes turned and her thoughts wandered to the place where the lady dressed in black was kneeling; and as soon as the " Missa est" was said, she rose and hurried toward the door, in order to be sure to get a view of her as she left the room. It was some time before the person she was watching stirred. At last, when she did so, she drew her veil over her face, and with a noiseless step glided through the door and down the stairs out of the hall door and into the street. Joan followed her closely, and, afraid of losing sight of her, caught hold of her dress. The face that turned round to look at her was as white as a sheet. The rough friendly grasp had been mist..ken for an arrest; but when the dark blue eyes of that wan and pallid visage met old Joan Porter's, such a ray of light shone in them as had not lighted them up for many a day. Mrs. Yates—for it was she—leaned breathless against the wall, looking the question she had not strength to utter.

"Yes, she's alive and well," Joan whispered; and then a flood of tears relieved the over-charged heart of the poor mother.

"Don't cry your heart out this way, ma'am; but come with me, and you will see our Polly."

"*He* will never see her—"

"Poor Mr. Yates, you mean? No, not in this bad world; but you'll all meet in heaven, which is better. Can you walk with me as far as Paddington to-night?"

"I don't know. O yes, anywhere, as long as

my limbs will carry me to see her. Is she—O Joan!—shall I really see her?"

"Of course you will. But·in the name of goodness, why haven't you written all this time, ma'am?"

"I have written. Did you not receive any letter from me?"

"Not a scrap of one."

"And no money?"

"No, never a bit."

"I never could send much, but once I trusted a person who was coming to England with a small sum he promised to deliver safely. We lived in such an out-of-the-way place—a small village miles distant from any high road, on the part of the coast where we were ship-wrecked."

"And how did you ever manage to get on there, ma'am?"

"Miserably enough. My husband became too ill to move; I could not leave him; and it was only by sending my trinkets to be sold at the nearest town that we obtained means of sub-sistence. At last he died, and all I had suffered before seemed as nothing compared to the anguish of that bereavement. But on the day he was laid in his humble grave, in the little cemetery of the village, I set off for England. As he was taken from me, my child was the only object I had to live for, and I half paid and half begged my way to England. But, Joan, I have no money to give to Mrs. Coggle, and I am ashamed to claim my child till I can pay what I owe her. Everything, you know, was taken from my husband, because after having been tempted in a weak moment to deny his faith, he retracted and boldly returned to the practice of his religion. I must work, and must earn money. I must repay all that has been spent on my Mary."

"Yes, yes, all in good time; I'll keep my mistress quiet about that. But do you come and fetch away your Polly, and take her home with you at once."

"Home!" Mrs. Yates repeated, in so sad a tone that the tears came into Joan's eyes. She felt all that that word conveyed of heart-breaking memories and actual desolation to the widowed mother. She longed to comfort her, but did not know how.

After a pause, Mrs. Yates said, "I will take a little room, however small, somewhere near where you live—"

"Yes, yes," Joan exclaimed, "that is the sensiblest thing that you have yet said."

"I will seek for needle-work, and by degrees—"

"O yes, degrees will do very well. Only fetch away Polly."

"Is she not happy — not well cared for?" Mrs. Yates anxiously asked.

"Lord bless you, yes, and only too much coddled by half. But she had best be with her own mother for all that. So you could not find us out?"

"No, I vainly inquired amongst your old neighbors.' One person gave me one direction —another, another; and it was in vain I went from place to place to try and find you."

"Then you will come soon?"

"This evening, after I have performed a sacred duty."

"Never mind sacred duties. The sacredest is to come to your child."

"I did not mean a religious duty, Joan. though indeed it is a holy duty in one sense—a debt of gratitude to be paid. A priest at St. Omer, who saved me from despair by his generous charity, has given me a message to take to his brother, who is in the Marshalsea, accused of having entered into the supposed plot for setting London on fire. The knowledge I can convey to him may preserve him from death, and save the property of many recusants."

"Let *me* go," Joan exclaimed; "I am used to the like secret contrivances, and do you go to Paddington. I am a better match any day, I take it, than you, ma'am, for the parliament, and gaolers, and the rest of them."

"No; nothing will make me consent to that. I have no fear for myself. It is not to the prison I am going, but to a place Father Sutton told me of, where I shall find some one who will take charge of the letter and convey it into the Marshalsea. So you see I run no risk, and this evening I hope to get to Paddington. Please give me your address. If you knew what I feel at the thoughts of seeing my little child! O, dear Joan, will she understand I am her mother?"

"Fast enough, I'll warrant you, as soon·as you show her a cross; and, by the way, here's your own, hidden here in my breast. But stop, I won't give it to you now, just as you are running your head into the lion's mouth; for this carrying of letters to priests, God bless them, is dangerous, and may end in ever so many mishaps."

"I should not have thought, Joan, that you would find it in your heart to dissuade me from an act which may save the life of one of God's servants. What would Doña Luisa have said?"

"Doña Luisa never was married, God bless her; and, as St. Paul says, that's the best state to be in, where you need no more care for your head being chopped off or your limbs quartered, than if you blew your nose; but if folk will marry and have children, then they should look after them as can't look after themselves. So do you give me that there letter."

"No, Joan; my mind is quite made up. I have a message to deliver as well as a letter. Pray that God may speed me on my way, and to-night—"

She wrung Joan's hand and walked quickly away. The old woman stood awhile looking after her, and then, as if rousing herself from a fit of painful abstraction, directed her own steps homewards.

CHAPTER IX.

A SLIP BETWEEN THE CUP AND THE LIP.

MANY a day had come and gone since the one on which Joan Porter had met Polly's mother in the chapel of the Spanish embassy, and talked to her afterwards in the street. She often asked herself if this brief interview had been a vision or a dream. For on the night of that interview, and for a long time afterwards, she had watched and waited for the coming of Mrs. Yates, and whenever the door opened expected to see her appear. But she never came, and the long silence that had preceded that sudden apparition was again renewed. Neither letter nor message relieved her anxiety. She had prudently forborne to mention to Mrs. Coggle on her return home that day that Polly's mother was in London, and was about to visit them and her child. She thought it would be better that she should be taken by surprise, and there-

fore held her tongue. But as her anxiety increased she gave hints on the subject which
were very ill received. She had come to the
end of her little savings, and had no longer
strength to walk great distances. So she could
neither make personal inquiries nor pay the
postage of letters. Poor Joan felt very sad and
very helpless. Polly was growing every day
more engaging, and learned her catechism so
well, and said her prayers so prettily, that any
one would have been proud of her. Lady
Davenant regularly sent the quarterly allow-
ance for the maintenance of her child, and for
all sorts of indulgences besides.

"She is a-stealing away of her heart," Joan
used to murmur, when these presents were
produced, and she had to use every art her art-
less nature could summon into play to counter-
act their effect on Polly. When she carried
her into the fields she took advantage of her
childish passion for buttercups and daisies, and
called them "mother's presents."

"Did mother make them?" Polly asked one
day. And Joan would reply, "No, but I am

5

sure she asks God to give them to Polly." And the same with the strawberries and the bunches of red and white currants which Joan begged for her darling from the market-woman. She always contrived to connect them with the thoughts of poor mother, who had such beautiful blue eyes and such soft white hands, and had so many kisses ready on her lips to give her child when she could come to her. Those little plans succeeded. "Tell about mother" was Polly's constant request when she sat on old Joan Porter's knees, watching the glowing embers in the winter, or the rosy clouds in the evening sky on the long summer days. And whenever she was taken by her devoted friend to one of the chapels of the foreign embassies, she immediately used to point to the pictures of the Blessed Virgin, and whisper, "That's mother." "Hush, don't talk now, there's a dear," Joan would answer. She was not perhaps very sorry that the thought of her mother in heaven and her mother on earth were sometimes blended in Polly's mind.

Nothing was heard of Mrs. Yates for five

years. Then one day a priest, whom Joan
happened to meet at a Catholic house where she
had gone to hear Mass, gave her a little note
written in pencil, which explained her disappear-
ance. She had been thrown into prison on the
very day Joan and she had met at Spanish Place,
on the charge of traitorously communicating
with a state prisoner. Notice had been given
to the pursuivants, of the house where some
noted Papists were looking to receive information from abroad, and a party of them were
watching near the door to arrest any one who
approached it. Mrs. Yates had no sooner
reached it than she found herself in the hands
of the pursuivants, and the letter she was carrying fell into their hands. She was consigned to
prison—kept in close confinement—forgotten
by every one, for she had no relatives and few
friends. For the first time she had managed
to obtain a scrap of paper, and with a bit of coal
had written a few lines to a priest she knew,
and begged him to communicate to Joan Porter
her sad history, and send her blessing to her
child. Poor Joan wiped her eyes, and said,

" I'm glad she isn't dead," and then went home and wondered how ever she might get to speak to her, and maybe help her out of prison. It seemed very hopeless. She was so infirm, and though she had done much for others in her day, she knew not where to find her friends; for the revival of persecution after the Fire of London had dispersed the most noted Catholics, and most of them had gone into the country or changed their abodes.

Mrs. Coggle would rather of the two that Mrs. Yates had been dead than in prison. She would then have felt quite easy in her mind, would have said, " Well, poor soul, she is at rest," and there would have been an end of it. As it was, she was really and sincerely sorry she was shut up, and yet dreadfully afraid she should come out. And she ended by declaring she did not believe that that scrap of paper meant anything, and she dared say it was all a mistake; and anyhow it was not their fault, which nobody had said it was; and so the matter rested, except that poor old Joan made fruitless efforts to convey letters and messages to the prisoner; and spent her last shilling, a lucky one with a hole in it, to bribe the turnkey to let her in. But it did not succeed, nor did her appeals to some Catholics who were supposed to be in favor at Court turn out as she had hoped. Some took no notice of her letters; others said it was no use to stir in the matter, or it was better not to remind people of this lady's existence, as she was in prison on a very serious charge, and might be tried for her life. When the Duke of York came to the throne there would be a better chance. Poor comforts, scanty hopes, heart-sickening delays! And meanwhile Polly was growing tall and slim, and very lovely. She was ten years old, and Joan had well instructed her in her religion, and, unknown to Mrs. Coggle, had been preparing her for her first communion. She had been to confession to a good old Jesuit Father, who had been Joan's own director for years, and who took a great interest in Mrs. Yates's child. On the next Easter Day, then close at hand, she was to have received the Bread of Angels, her Lord and her God, in her young heart. It always seems

strange to our limited views when a holy
purpose is frustrated; when some grace long
prayed for and waited for is withheld at the
very moment when our hopes are highest and
our desires most ardent; when what it is right
intensely to wish for is denied, and our prayers
appear to be flatly rejected instead of granted.
Joan had passionately longed for the hour when
Mrs. Yates's child was to approach the altar for
the first time. She counted the days and then
the hours till that hour should arrive. It was
actually to be on the next morning. She had
planned everything so as to avoid Mrs. Coggle's
observation or interference, and foresaw no difficulty in the accomplishment of the cherished
hope of her heart. Polly sat on her knees,
though rather old for that now, and asked for
her mother's cross.

"Dear Joan," she said, "may I wear it to-
morrow whilst I am in the chapel? We can
hide it under my kerchief till we get upstairs."

It was upstairs, in a house a little way off
from the one where they lived, that a small
garret served as a chapel. It was there a few

Catholics met on great festivals to hear Mass and approach the Sacraments. It was there they had to go at break of day, before any one in the neighborhood was stirring.

"Why, yes," Joan said; "you shall wear it, my dear; and look what I've got for you here. Some one as I know brought this letter an hour ago. I had prayed hard for some means to let your mother know that to-morrow you are to make your first communion. The angels must have helped us, for, lo and behold, I met this person yesterday, and he said to me, 'I've a chance to speak to a prisoner in the Marshalsea. Have you any friend there, Mistress Porter, as you'd like to send a greeting to?' My heart jumped into my mouth, and sure enough I told him what to say to one Mrs. Yates, and this morning he gives me this here paper—your mother's own writing—my precious one. See what she says."

On a tiny bit of paper was written in a minute hand what St. Theresa once wrote in her breviary. It seemed, perhaps, a singular choice the mother had made of these sentences to con-

gratulate her young child on her first communion ; but she was perhaps inspired to select
them.

"Let nothing trouble thee,
Let nothing affright thee.
All things pass away.
    God never changes.
Patience obtains everything,
Nothing is wanting to him
Who possesses God.
    God alone suffices."

Polly read them, and said, " I will let nothing
affright me, Joan, whatever happens."

An hour afterwards, a lady and gentleman
called, and begged to see Mrs. Coggle. They
announced themselves as friends of Lady Davenant's, and produced a letter from her, in which
she begged that her young daughter should be
given up to Mr. and Mistress Brydone, who at
her request had made all the necessary arrange-
ments for removing her to a seminary at Richmond, where her education was to be carried on.
They were in London only for a very few days,
which would account for the suddenness of this
announcement. Rose Davenant was to proceed
with them at once to her new home, where

she would be trained in a manner befitting her birth and fortune. Mrs. Coggle might visit her there whenever she thought fit, and Lady Davenant would continue to that lady for life the pension she had paid while her child was under her care. She was glad thus to testify her sense of the excellent way in which Mrs. Coggle had performed the duties she had undertaken.

"A pension for life!" this was indeed more than the widow had expected. Such handsome thanks too—and Polly, that was to say Rose, to be educated as a young lady of high rank! It was all good news, if only—O, if only Joan had been out of the house! Not that she could stand out against her, and against Lady Davenant's friends, but perhaps she would try and make all sorts of unpleasantness. Necessity, or even a difficulty, stimulates invention. Mrs. Coggle, with the courage of despair, begged the gentlefolk to sit down awhile in her parlor, while she slipped out and got a prescription out of the cupboard of her bedroom, which she carried to Joan, who was at that moment superintending the girl in the kitchen.

" Joan," she cried in an agitated voice, " please to step out with this here prescription to the chemist. I am taken all on a sudden so ill in myself, that I want this medicine made up directly, there's my good Joan; and wait, I beg of you, if it be ever so long, while it is making, for them boys as they send out with the physic never do bring it till the next day."

Joan made no reply, but took down her cloak, put on her bonnet, and in another moment was out of the house.

When Mrs. Coggle returned to the parlor, a load was off her mind; she said, " Now, I suppose you would like to see—Miss Davenant?"

" Yes, and if it is not inconvenient to you, we will take her away with us at once, and a cart will call in the evening for her luggage."

Mrs. Coggle stood irresolutely, with the handle of the door in her hand. " Must she go at once?" she asked.

" Indeed, I think we must beg of you to let her do so, for we have no time to spare, and are anxious to report to Lady Davenant that her wishes have been carried out."

"But I hope," Mrs. Brydone exclaimed, "that she won't cry and fret at parting with you, for that sort of thing makes me positively ill."

"I'll tell you what, ma'am," Mrs. Coggle cried; suppose you say you are taking her out for an airing, and then Joan and I can go and see her to-morrow. We'll hire the grocer's cart, he does not use it every day; and so the dear lamb won't feel the parting so much. You'll be sure and say, when you leave her at the school, that we shall ride to Richmond for to see her to-morrow."

"Well, perhaps that will be the best way," Mrs. Brydone said, "and if you can get her bonneted and cloaked, we can set out directly."

A few moments afterwards the little girl came in, blushing deeply at the thoughts of a ride in a fine coach with a gentleman and lady. Mrs. Coggle could hardly keep from crying; but interest on the one hand, and the fear of Joan on the other, made her hurry to the conclusion which, sooner or later, she knew must be inevitable. "And it's no long parting either," she said to herself, as she stood at the door watching the carriage drive away, which Polly had entered under the full belief that she was only taken out for an hour's ride.

There are actions which people have a vague feeling at their hearts are wrong, and yet they do not quite see why they should be so, taking for granted their own view of the case. Polly was just as much Rose Davenant as Polly Yates. Mrs. Coggle had always said so; and here was her live mother, who had a right to her, claiming her child: and what for but to make a lady of her, and all of them comfortable for all their lives, and to give her a fine education, and no parting, for to speak of, from the dear child? She went upstairs to pack up the child's clothes, and somehow all the little odds and ends that filled her drawers seemed to reproach her with this sudden departure. There was her doll that she was so fond of; would they let her have it at school, she wondered? Anyhow they would take it to her the next day. And then the spelling-book, in which she had made her first studies, and the primer, half-finished, in a little basket. Poor Mrs. Coggle began to feel more and more sad, and when at last she heard Joan's voice on the stairs, she actually trembled, and felt as much frightened as if she had murdered the child. She had not realized what it would be to have to tell Joan that Polly was gone. When she did so, when the poor old woman, whose thoughts had been dwelling on the child's first communion as the consummation of ten years' incessant devotion, love, and prayer, heard, and at last understood, that her darling—the child of the poor, imprisoned Catholic mother—had been given up to strangers and to Protestants, was severed from the means of grace and the practice of her religion, her agony was so great, that though it only found vent in the words, "God forgive you, mistress; you don't know what you've done!" there was an expression in her face which frightened the widow.

"O Joan," she exclaimed, "you are not going for to die!"

"No, ma'am," Joan answered; "if I can, I'll live, please God, to save her."

She sat some time wrapt in thought, feeling the whole bitterness of her grief, measuring the impossibility of recovering the child, save by incessant prayers that God would find the means and bring about the end. Joan was endowed with the highest degree of practical good sense. She never did anything useless, but never left undone anything possible. She did not lament or upbraid after the first expression of her grief and indignation. She held her peace, and when she went to see Polly the next day, and the child, throwing herself into her arms, clung wildly to her, with passionate entreaties to be taken home, and whispered cries that she hated the Protestant prayers, and would always be a Catholic, she did not indulge in any outburst of feeling, but uttered a few words that sunk deeply into the young heart beating so wildly against her aged breast—such words as God puts into the mouth of the humble of heart and strong in faith when they are struggling, like guardian angels, to save souls committed to their charge by a nameless trust, or rather a secret Providence.

CHAPTER X.

THE BOARDING-SCHOOL AT RICHMOND.

On one of those lovely afternoons of an English summer, at the hour when the lights and shades on the grass and amongst the foliage impart the greatest charm to woodland scenery, what is more beautiful than Richmond, and the view from its glorious terrace? The very name of it awakens a vision hardly to be surpassed in nature or in art: the hill, the park, the bridge, the bright glassy river; the masses of green above and beneath, and spreading out as far as the eye can reach—the soft blue sky, and the white fleecy clouds casting their shadows on the stream and on the mead. Each time that after a long interval we stand again on the height above that smiling scene, its beauty takes us by surprise. In the days we are writing of, it looked different in many respects from what it does now. It lacked most of the villas that line

the margin of the Thames. The town itself, and
the green, comprised most of the habitable
houses, and there was still something primeval
in the woods that separated it from the adjoin-
ing villages of Petersham and Twickenham.

Mrs. Dimple's boarding-school was situated
between the green and the river. It was a large
red brick house, with gable ends; the garden
had wide alleys, lined with trees, and a maze,
which formed the delight of the younger schol-
ars. In a long, low room, extending from one
end of the building to the other, on a lovely
afternoon in June, some of the older pupils were
assembled, and occupied with needle-work—
which formed at that period a more important
part of a girl's education than it does at present.
Their tongues did not rest while their fingers
were employed; and the following conversation
took place during Mrs. Dimple's momentary
absence from the work-table.

Fanny Marchbanks asked Jane Caldwell if she
had seen a huge parcel of cakes and sweetmeats
which Emma Robson had received from her
aunt—which drew forth the remark, that girls

whose relatives lived in the country were those who received most nice things in the course of the year. Ann Dawson said that Rose Davenant was the best off of all in that respect. She got from France large cases, filled with flat baked apples and dried plums, and ever so many rare biscuits.

Upon this, Jane remarked that Rose Davenant was a queer girl. Bessie Fairchild looked up indignantly from her embroidery, and exclaimed that Rose was the nicest girl in the school, and she saw nothing queer about her. Jane retorted that at any rate a queer body came to see her. That old woman, with a nightcap and a great umbrella, who looked for all the world like a Jack-in-the-Green or a Guy Fawkes. For her part, she wondered that Rose —if she was a lady's daughter—should spend her holidays in a mean part of the suburbs with two old women, who were neither kith nor kin to her. Ann said, that the only time she had ever seen Rose in a passion was when some of the girls giggled at the sight of Mistress Porter's dress.

"Well, I wonder," rejoined Jane, "why her mother — whom one would think doted on her, by the lots of presents she receives—does not send for her home to where she lives in France. Bessie may say what she pleases, but I declare there's something uncommon about that girl."

"I never said there wasn't," Bessie warmly rejoined. "I think there is something uncommonly good and uncommonly nice about her. Don't you think so, Fanny?"

Before Fanny could answer, Jane exclaimed, "I'm sure she thinks her queer."

"Well, Jane, if it is queer to be always ready to do a kindness, and always to speak the truth, even if one should have to suffer for it, I'll grant you Rose is queer."

Ann admitted that she was very good about not telling tales, and would often help girls with their lessons at a pinch.

"Ah, but you don't know what I've found out," Jane said, in a kind of impressive whisper, which commanded general attention; and once secure of this, she said in the same tone, "She

wears a cross, which she hides in her dress. I
have seen her kiss it, too. She'll be in an awful
scrape, if Mrs. Dimple finds her out."

"You don't think she is a Papist?" Ann
asked, in a horrified voice.

"I'll tell you what," Jane said, "if she is not
one, the old woman who comes to see her is
as rank a one as ever lived. The new parlor
maid says so."

"Dear me," Ann ejaculated, "how very
strange! I shall look at her closely the next
time she pays Rose a visit. I wonder what
Papists are like?"

At that moment the door opened, and the
young girl who had always been called Rose
Davenant at Mrs. Dimple's school came into the
room. She was tall and very pretty: her countenance expressive, and her manner engaging.
Even those of her companions who had been
speaking of her disparagingly seemed to feel
the influence of that peculiarly winning manner.
She came in with a box of chocolate in her hand,
and offered some to all the girls, till the contents
were exhausted.

"You have kept none for yourself," Bessie said, in a low voice.

"I don't care for it," was the smiling answer. Then she turned to Jane Caldwell, and said, in a kind way, "You look tired, Jane."

"I am tired to death of this stitching," Jane replied. "I am a horribly slow worker, and never get to the end of my task in time. It is a horrid bore, for the girls are going into the park this evening, and I shall be kept at home if this is not finished."

Rose eagerly stretched out her hand, and said,

"Let me finish it. I had an easy piece of work to do to-day, which took me a very short time. I shall like to go on with yours."

Bessie Fairchild, who was sitting next to Jane, whispered to her,

"She is a queer girl, is not she?"

Jane pretended not to hear; allowed Rose to take her work from her, and leaned her head against the top of her high-backed chair with a look of considerable satisfaction.

Ann Dawson observed that the chocolate

was excellent, and asked if it came from France.

Rose nodded assent, and Fanny asked her if she was not longing to go to France.

"If I were you, I should be dying for it," she said.

"Have you never seen your mother?" one of the girls inquired, who had not been long at the school.

Rose did not answer at once, and bent down, as if to look for her needle.

"I wonder why you don't go home for the holidays?" Jane said, rocking herself backwards and forwards on her chair.

"If you knew anything of geography," Fanny said, "you would know that it takes more time to go to Montpellier and back than the holidays last."

"It must be so odd never to see one's mother!" Jane rejoined; upon which Bessie waxed very wrath, and said to her, in an angry manner:

"Don't you see that you are vexing Rose by your foolish talk? You have no business to make such remarks."

" Mind your own business, and don't preach to me!" was the rejoinder. " I have a right to say what I please. It is not my fault if a girl is so thin-skinned that she can't bear to hear a simple remark like that."

"If I were you, Rose," Fanny cried out, "I would not do another stitch of Jane's work. She is very ill-natured."

" I did not begin to speak of her mother, and I'm sure I did not ask her to help me," Jane exclaimed.

" No, you did not," Rose said, making a strong effort over herself, and speaking good-humoredly; "and you did not mean to vex or tease me. You wanted to rest, and I wanted something to do—so it was all right, and as it should be."

This conciliatory speech produced a happy effect, and all went on peaceably. At the striking of the clock, Mrs. Dimple, the very picture of a school-mistress of that day, made her appearance, and gave orders that the young ladies who had finished their task should rise and prepare for their evening walk. When she perceived that Rose did not move, and continued to work, she commented on the propriety of the regulations that deprived of their recreation those young ladies who idled over their tasks. She uttered some just though rather prosy sentiments on the merits of diligence, and observed neither Jane's uncomfortable look of consciousness, nor the fact that Bessie had unpicked some of the stitches at the end of her strip of muslin, in order not to appear to have finished her task, and so to attain to the enviable privilege of spending an hour in the quiet, deserted school-room with Rose, whom she worshipped with all the enthusiasm of a girlish affection. The stratagem succeeded. The workboxes were closed one by one, the young ladies left the room, Mrs. Dimple at their head, and then the door was shut. Two chairs moved to the window, where the two friends sat enjoying the perfume of the lime blossoms, the singing of the birds, the cool air blowing in upon them from the river, and the intense pleasure of being together and communicating freely their pent-up thoughts. Justice had been blind on this as

on other occasions, and her ends had been ful-
filled; for Rose, as she was called at school, and
her faithful ally, Bessie Fairchild, had not
deserved punishment, and enjoyed what they
both looked upon as a great pleasure. The
following conversation took place between
them.

"I am so glad we are alone," Bessie said,
with a sigh of relief. "I want to know if you
have seen Joan lately."

"Not for a long time. I wish she would
come, or write to me. She is not much of a
scholar, Joan, and it takes her a great deal of
trouble to pen a letter. You are the only one
in the world, Bess, besides Joan, to whom I can
speak of what I am always thinking of."

"You mean your two mothers, and which is
the real one?"

"Yes, it is so passing strange to receive
letters, such very different ones, and such kind
ones, from two persons both calling themselves
my mother, and not to know which is really
my own."

"Mrs. Dimple always calls Lady Davenant your mother, and so does your Mrs. Coggle."

" Yes, but Joan does not ; and I am inclined to think she knows best."

" Which of them has written to you last ? "

" O, Lady Davenant. She writes very often, and on fine thin paper, which smells of perfume. She calls me her sweet Rose, and promises in her last letter that I shall soon live with her in a beautiful house, go out into society, and enjoy the pleasures and gayeties of the world."

" Does she really ? What a change that will be from this dull life at school ! Don't you like the thoughts of it ? "

" Yes, in a sort of way ; but it frightens me, too, to think of it. Joan has told me so often, since I was quite a little child, that we are not to love the world nor the things of this world. How shall I help doing so if I am to live in it, and enjoy all its pleasures ? Even in the catechism we learn here we are made to say that at our baptism we renounced all the pomps and vanities of this world."

" Yes, I know ; and yet every girl here is
6

longing for the time when she shall be finely dressed, and go to balls and assemblies."

"I have heard very seldom from my other mother, Mrs. Yates—only six or seven times during the many years I have been at school. Her letters are written on coarse bits of paper, and appear to be written with a bad pen, or rather with the stump of one. This is the last I received from her; I always carry it about with me."

"O, do let me read it."

"I will read it to you. The handwriting is difficult to make out, but I know every word of it by heart. It is very short.

"'MY DEAREST MARY,—I am hardly able to write at all times, and cannot say all I should wish. I lack the means of doing so, and must take such as present themselves, thanking God that I can send even these few lines. To Him I commend thee, my precious one, praying that He may have thee in His keeping, and that my child may learn to wait, to pray, and even, if it should be His will, to suffer, like her poor loving mother.'"

" O, what a sad letter!" Bessie exclaimed.

" Well, it does not make me feel sad. I have indeed shed many tears over it; but when I press it this way against my heart, it seems to make it burn with the love of God."

" What a strange way of talking that is! One never hears any of the clergymen speak of that sort of thing."

" No, indeed, there is not much warmth in their sermons. One of Joan Porter's short teachings, when we are left a moment alone, is worth all their preachings put together in that respect."

" Where does Mrs. Yates write from?"

" The letter does not say; but if you will promise not to tell anybody, I will confide to you a secret about her."

" I promise I won't. You know, Rose, I always keep my promises. I never said anything about your cross; but that odious Jane has found out that you have one."

" Don't call people odious, dear Bess. You know what our Lord says of those who use words of that sort."

"You are so strict, Rose. All the girls do so, more or less. But now tell me about Mrs. Yates."

"Well, Bessie, she is a Catholic, a Roman Catholic, and has been shut up a long time in prison, because she would not betray the name of a priest to whom she had brought a letter. She was arrested, Joan says, with that letter upon her, the very day when she was coming to fetch me away from Mrs. Coggle's house, ten years ago."

"What, has she been all that time shut up?"

"Yes. Joan says she would have been released long ago if she would have given the name of the priest. But she would not do it. I think it is so brave of her. It is being a martyr, or at any rate something like it. Joan said the last time I saw her that she had some hopes now she would soon be set free. A good Protestant gentleman is working very hard about it."

"Does Mrs. Dimple know that Joan is a Catholic?"

"I am not sure. She seems lately to take great care not to leave us much alone together."

"But if she knew it, she would not let her come here at all."

"I am not so sure of that. Mrs. Dimple has a kind heart."

"Well, I know that she had me whipped when I first came here because I said I was a Catholic."

"But was it true, Bessie, that you were one?"

"I was till my father and mother died; then my uncle sent me here, and said I was to be a Protestant."

"Well, I'll tell you something. I am not so much afraid about Jane's knowing about my having a cross, because Mrs. Dimple found it out some months ago."

"How ever did you let her see it?"

"Well, I was not very well last winter. I had a bad cold, and was lying awake one evening when the other girls in our room were fast asleep. I had taken my cross into my hands. I often do when I am not sleeping. All at once I saw Mrs. Dimple standing by my bedside with a basin of caudle in one hand and a candle in the other. She had come in so softly that I had not heard her. Directly, I saw that she had taken notice of my cross. But she said nothing, only told me to drink what she had brought for my cold, and try to go to sleep. Well, two or three days afterwards she sent for me to her own parlor. You know how one's heart beats when that happens. She looked dreadfully grave when I went in, and began in the voice you know: " Young lady, you have on your person or in your box a forbidden, treasonable, and dangerous possession, which I require you at once to place in my hands, in order that it may be dealt with according to the laws of this country and of this school. I ought to inflict upon you a severe chastisement, which would yet be mild in comparison with what the magistrates would award you should your offence come to their knowledge; but this time you shall be pardoned, providing you promise not to repeat the offence." I stood silent a moment, and then I said, " Madam, my heart will break if you take from me the cross which my mother gave me; but to resign it voluntarily I never will, whatever punishment may be inflicted on me." .

" She looked at me steadily, and said, ' Truly, did your mother give you that graven image, and is your value for it founded on your love for her?' I answered not the first question, because, although I should have spoken the truth in mine own thoughts, I might have been, later on, charged by her with falsehood; but I said boldly, 'Madam, I do value it, first and chiefly for the love of Him who is represented on that cross, and died thereon for each of us, and afterwards, also, for a meaner love, insomuch as it is earthly.' She said nothing, but opened my dress, and cutting its string, laid hold of my cross. O Bessie! God only knows how, from a baby, I have prized it, and when I have missed all other comfort, found it in this likeness of Christ our Lord. I said nothing, but the sudden sinking of my heart was, I think, expressed in my countenance, for our mistress relented. She hesitated a little; then, emboldened, I spoke: 'O mistress, I have been orphaned of the care of a parent from my earliest infancy. Take not from me what has often stood me in the stead of what I lost thereby.' After a moment's silence, she said, 'You have learned in the history of Greece how the young Spartans were publicly chastised if discovered doing that which nevertheless might be otherwise commendable. If you continue to keep this keepsake, since it is such, from the eyes of your school-fellows, it may remain with you; but if you should be known to have it, public disgrace and punishment will follow;' and so I was dismissed, with more love in my heart toward our mistress than I had, ever felt before."

"But now you are in the power of that ill-natured Jane, who may inform the mistress of it, as she did just now the other girls."

"Well, then, I must bear the punishment; and even so, I do not think the cross will be taken from me. You see, Mrs. Dimple thinks it is Lady Davenant who gave it me. But, Bessie dear, are you still in heart a Catholic?"

"So much so that I say a 'Hail Mary' every

day, and would not like to go to sleep without it."

" So do I, and I always make the sign of the cross under my tippet. Joan keeps me up to it, and says it would break my mother's heart if I were actually to turn Protestant."

" Then you do really think Mrs. Yates is your mother, and not Lady Davenant?"

" From what Joan tells me I am sure of it, and something in my heart persuades me it is so."

" Did you hear that knock at the door?"

" Yes, and I heard just now the carriage wheels in the road. I hope it is some of Mrs. Dimple's own friends."

" Why so?"

" O, because she will then sup with them in her own parlor, and we shall be more free this evening."

" How nice the air from the river is! Don't you like to hear that rustling in the trees when the evening breeze begins to blow? There, I have finished Jane's work. Is yours done?"

" All but one stitch."

" Do you think we might walk in the garden
a little, as we have finished our tasks?"

The door opened just as Rose was asking
that question, and a maid said, " Miss Davenant,
you are requested to come into the parlor."

" Is Mrs. Coggle there? or dear old Joan?"
Rose cried eagerly, springing forward.

" No, Miss, neither one nor the other, somebody very different.   But I have been forbidden
to mention who."

Rose's heart began to beat violently.   " It is
one of them," she said to herself—"which?   I
must wash my hands before I go to the parlor,"
she said, hastily running past the maid.   Once
in the dormitory, she locked the door, knelt for a
moment by her bedside, kissed her little crucifix,
and then having bathed her face and hands in
cold water, walked slowly down-stairs, feeling as
if there was a mist before her eyes.

CHAPTER XI.

LADY DAVENANT was not much changed by the twelve years that had passed over her head. She was still a very pretty woman, was dressed in the extreme of the fashion of her day, which was a very becoming one. There was a sunny smile on her face and a sprightliness in her manner which could not fail to be engaging. She was sitting by Mrs. Dimple's side when the young girl whom she looked upon as her daughter came into the room. She rose with extended arms, and cried,

"O my Rose! my child! this is indeed a happy moment."

It was somewhat in accordance with the habits of the time that she who was thus addressed, instead of rushing into those open arms, made a low obeisance, seized one of the lady's hands, and kissing it, said,

"Dear honored madam, how kind you are!"

Lady Davenant raised the kneeling girl, pressed her to her breast, and then made her sit by her side, keeping one of her hands in hers. She looked at her with evident satisfaction. Even in her simple school dress she looked lovely. It was a peculiar style of beauty, not much color in her face, but a delicate white complexion; regular features, and wonderfully beautiful eyes, made her exactly what Lady Davenant would have wished, except in one respect. She saw at once that she was not the least like herself. Perhaps there shot across her mind at that instant a sort of doubt, which would not have even arisen had she been rosy and dazzlingly fair; but it was no more than a passing thought, instantly dismissed. Still holding her hand, she turned to Mrs. Dimple and said:

"I have so long looked forward to this day; I really thought poor dear Mr. Mordaunt would never depart this life. I have been a perfect slave to him, especially since he lost his sight. If I had left his side even for one month he would, I doubt not, have changed his will, and left his fortune to a Mrs. Yates, the widow of his nephew. He had disinherited them because they were Papists; but sometimes he used, when he was out of temper with me, to speak of them as his heirs. After George Yates's death, he lost all knowledge of her, but often wondered if he had left children. Once he dictated to me some inquiries on the subject, and sent the letter to a friend in England, but it received no answer. You may imagine what an anxious life I led, and how impossible it was for me to absent myself. However, all is well that ends well, as the great dramatist says. I have inherited all his fortune, and can take this dear child, who I see at once does high credit to your tuition, to a house which she will enjoy, I hope, as much as myself. We shall lead a very agreeable life, Rose, I promise you. Lady and Miss Davenant will appear at Court next winter and astonish the gay world. But I see tears in your eyes. I hope you are crying for joy."

Rose blushed deeply, and answered,

" Your goodness, dear madam, exceeds all I

could have expected, even after the many past favors I have received from you. But I am bewildered at the prospect of so sudden and great a change; and then, I am not, I fear, what you would wish me to be, in more ways than one."

"On the contrary, my dear," Lady Davenant replied, "I commend highly your humility; but I assure you that I am very much pleased with your appearance, and when you are dressed according to my fancy--in the style, I mean, in which my friend Sir Peter Lely paints the beauties of the Court—your good looks will be much enhanced. Your eyes are fine, and with a little rouge and a few patches the whiteness of your complexion will show to great advantage. Do you play on any musical instrument?"

"On the guitar, madam," Rose timidly answered.

"She has a pretty talent for music, and dances very gracefully. Her disposition is truly amiable, and her heart affectionate."

Mrs. Dimple's voice showed some emotion as she uttered those last words. Rose had

always been one of her favorite pupils, and she
was touched by her tears, which she ascribed to
sorrow at leaving school—a tribute seldom paid
to it by the young ladies on their final departure.

Some farther conversation passed, and then
Rose, after a tender embrace from Lady Davenant, was dismissed, and sent to her companions,
with permission to tell them that in three days
she was to leave school, and that on the eve
of her departure a whole holiday would be
granted, and a parting feast held under the
trees in the park, in honor of Lady Davenant's
arrival.

The walking party had not yet returned, and
Rose (for we are forced for the time being so to
call her) found her faithful friend Bessie waiting for her in a perfect fever of curiosity and
suspense.

"Well, Rose, is she—I mean, what is she like?
What does she say?"

Rose had thrown herself on the seat near the
window, covered her face with her hands, and
burst into an agony of tears. Poor Bessie stood

looking at her with something of that eager wistful look which we see in attached dogs when some one they love is crying.

"O dear me, dear me! do tell me about it. The girls will be home directly, and we may not have, for ever so long, an opportunity of talking."

"I don't know what to say, or to think, or to feel," Rose passionately exclaimed. "She has no doubt of my being her child—she is kindness itself. She is going to take me away in three days."

"O dear! O dear! I thought it would be so, but go on," poor Bessie said; "I don't mind, if only you are happy, and it's all right."

"But that's just what it isn't, all right. I don't feel a bit as if she were my mother. My heart does not warm toward her, and I am afraid of the life she holds out in prospect to me. The world, the Court, gayety, pleasure; not one word did she say about—"

"About what?"

"About being good, and God, and all that sort of thing. O Bessie, what shall I do? I

have no one to advise me; if only I could see
Joan! I know what I shall do; I will write and
beg her to come here the day after to-morrow.
I wonder if she could get my letter in time?
The carrier will take it to-morrow morning to
London, and post it there. I am afraid, unless
it went by private hand, she would not get it
for two days, and I am sure Mrs. Dimple will
not help me to send it. I want to know if I
ought to tell Lady Davenant about Mrs. Yates
thinking that I am her child—I don't know if
it would be right or wrong—and also that I
want to be a Catholic. I was in a mortal fright
lest Mrs. Dimple should speak about my cross.
It is like being a hypocrite to be kissing Lady
Davenant, and thanking her, and all the time
saying to myself, 'I don't believe you are my
mother.' Not but that I ought to thank her,
for she has had me brought up all this time as
if I were her daughter, and paid for my board
and schooling. Do you think I ought to tell
her?"

"But if she *is* your mother, it will be undutiful in you to go and say you don't think so, and

it will make her hate you, perhaps; and it is only Joan and those dirty bits of paper that say so. If I were you, I'd make up my mind she is, and then you'll love her directly, and be very happy."

"No, I shall never be happy that way; but perhaps you are right, and that I had better not speak of my doubts till I am sure I ought to do so. Well, I'll say nothing now. I'll go away with her on Thursday; be very good and quiet, and talk very little; only kiss her when she kisses me, and so on. Then, when we are in London, I shall ask her to let me ride in her coach to Paddington, to see Mrs. Coggle and Joan. As she is so rich, she must have plenty of horses and servants; and then, if only I can see Joan, I shall know what to do."

At that moment Lady Davenant came into the class-room to take another farewell of her daughter, spoke of the feast she was going to give to her dear Rose's school-fellows, asked if Bessie was her favorite companion, and invited her to spend the next holidays at her house.

This kindness went to the hearts of the two girls, and when the door was closed upon her, Bessie exclaimed,

" Now, Rose, if that is not the best and kindest mother that any one could wish to have! If I were you, I would throw away all those scraps of letters which mean nothing at all, and let old Joan Porter say what she likes about Mrs. Yates. Do you stick to Lady Davenant, whom I declare is the handsomest and best-spoken lady in the world. And what fun we shall have in the holidays! I was to have spent them, as usual, in this dull, hateful house. I can't think how such a piece of luck has come to me."

" Don't make too sure of this prospect, dear Bess," Rose said, somewhat sadly, "and don't call this house hateful. We have known many a happy hour under these old trees, been carefully and tenderly nursed in sickness, and sheltered from many a temptation by the care we have had here."

" O yes; you think of that because you

are going away. You forget the tasks, the punishments, the scoldings, and all the torments of school. You are a very happy girl now."

Rose's heart swelled. She had few friends, and the friend of her school days, the only one of her own age she cared for, proved herself utterly incapable of understanding, not only the extent, but the nature of her sufferings. It was a relief to her that the return of the other girls just then interrupted their conversation; but she had soon to endure the shouts of delight which followed the announcement of the whole holiday, granted at Lady Davenant's request, and could not escape the flood of questions, exclamations, and congratulations which followed. There is not a more painful feeling than that of being the object of envy to all around us when we are oppressed with a grief or an anxiety which cannot be disclosed. When her head was laid on the pillow, and silence and darkness spread their soothing influence over her soul, then did those words

which had comforted her on the first night
she had spent in that house return to her
mind, like a whisper from her guardian
angel :

> " Let nothing trouble thee,
> Let nothing affright thee ;
> All things pass away.
>   God never changes."

CHAPTER XII.

DAVENANT HOUSE.

THE house in London which had belonged to
Mr. Mordaunt, and had once more come into
Lady Davenant's possession, was now furnished
and adorned in a costly manner. It was agree-
ably situated not far from the Temple Buildings,
facing the river, and with a garden sloping to
its banks. The drive from Richmond in a
coach-and-four, the arrival at this mansion,
which surpassed in splendor anything she had
ever witnessed, the liveried servants in the hall,
and the whole aspect of her future abode, filled
with amazement the young girl so suddenly
introduced into a scene of such comfort and
luxury. The dreamlike feeling this transition
produced was increased when Lady Davenant,
after leading her through the reception rooms,
conducted her dear Rose to what she said was
to be her own room. She had never had one of
her own before.

Joan Porter's dingy bedchamber at Paddington and the dormitory at school were her only
conceptions of a sleeping apartment, and now
she was actually given to understand that this
stately chamber, with its canopied bed, its gilt
mirrors, its high-backed chairs, its toilet-table,
its wardrobe, and its two windows with seats,
which overlooked the garden and the river,
was actually her own. It seemed like a new
world, and she was glad when Lady Davenant
went away and she found herself alone, free to
muse on her position and collect her agitated
thoughts. It was some time before she could
bring them into any shape. Was this, the
splendor, the brightness which suddenly surrounded her, a dream? or was this the reality,
and those remembrances of the past—those
tidings, few and far between, rare as angels'
visits, from within the walls of a prison, of
another mother than the one that now claimed
her—an unearthly vision then fading away in
darkness and oblivion? If only she could feel
toward Lady Davenant as a child toward a
parent! Perhaps she might arrive at it in time,

especially if Joan Porter encouraged her to do so, and would let her give up thinking of Mrs. Yates. "If I were to give her back this cross and these letters, and try to believe I am Lady Davenant's daughter?" But no sooner did this idea cross her mind than she burst into tears, kissed the little crucifix, read over the letters, and felt all the old feelings of reverence for the Catholic religion and her Catholic mother, which Joan had instilled into her, re-asserting their power. There was a prie-dieu in one corner of the room, with a finely-bound Book of Common Prayer lying on it. She quietly displaced the volume, laid her cross on the velvet cushion, fetched from the chimney two vases full of flowers, and placed them on each side of it, in remembrance of what she had seen in the chapels she used to go to with Joan. There she knelt down, and whilst gaz-ing on the nailed hands and pierced feet and thorn-crowned brow of her Divine Lord, she felt an irresistible gush of tender yearning for the parent who for so many years had been praying for her, as one of her short letters said, that she might always be a true child of God's Church.

A noise in the passage interrupted this train of thought. A waiting-woman appeared, sent by her ladyship to assist Miss Davenant to dress. The heavenly dream faded away. The earthly reality resumed its power. It was pleasant to be attired in beautiful clothes, and to be told how admirably they became her; and that the yellow silk gown, which would have ill suited Lady Davenant's fair hair and florid complexion, set off quite marvellously her daughter's different style of beauty. The result of the waiting-woman's labor was highly successful, and her mistress's smile of pleasure when Rose came into the drawing-room showed how pleased she was with the result.

Guests came to dinner, and were presented to the young lady of the house. Each time that Lady Davenant said "My daughter" a painful sensation came over the so-called Rose. It seemed so false to accept this position and to receive compliments which an inward voice in her heart protested she was not entitled to.

7

Her silence and her blushes were ascribed to the novelty of the scene and an excess of charming timidity, which in one so beautiful only enhanced her girlish attractions.

Amongst Lady Davenant's visitors that day was a young gentleman, the expectant heir of a large fortune, who had been brought to her house by his father, Sir Mark Le Grange, for the express purpose of making the acquaintance of that lady's only daughter. Sir Mark and Lady Davenant had met in Paris when she was on her way home from Montpellier, and the subject of a marriage between his son and her daughter had been broached. The match appeared on both sides highly desirable. Sir Mark had large landed estates, and Lady Davenant was prepared to give her daughter an ample dowry. Parents, when they agreed on a project of this sort, did not anticipate, in those days, much opposition on the part of their children, and it was not in this instance likely that the young gentleman would object to so fair a bride as his father had selected for him or the young lady to the handsome and amiab:

youth her mother had chosen for her future husband. Lady Davenant, had, however, stipulated that Rose should not be married for one year after leaving school, and in the meantime Mr. Le Grange was to travel on the Continent and improve his knowledge of foreign languages. A previous interview was, however, to take place, and the day assigned for it was that which followed Lady Davenant's return to London. On the morrow Mr. Le Grange was to go abroad. His eyes were well satisfied with the face and figure of the young lady proposed to him as a wife, but it was not till after dinner, during a walk in St. James's Park, that he had an opportunity of conversing with her. What they said to each other is not much to the purpose. It was probably nothing very striking or brilliant, but that a mutual satisfaction was felt in the exchange of those few words was evident. Something in Miss Davenant's countenance and manner, and in her timid answers to the remarks he made, caused Mr. Le Grange inwardly to rejoice that his father had chosen for him better than he could have chosen for himself, and she was of opinion that although he was the only young man she had ever conversed with, a more courteous and agreeable one could not exist. The park was full that day of gay company. There was music under the trees and there were games on the lawn. The evening breeze, after a hot day, felt refreshing and sweet, and in the midst of this cheerful scene and pleasant society Rose began again to doubt if she was bound to break the web that was encircling her round. The next day it seemed to be hemming her in yet more closely, for Lady Davenant asked her if she had seen anything she disliked in the person or the manners of the young Mr. Le Grange; and on her answering by a blushing negative, said she was glad, and hoped that she would not object to oblige her by accepting him as a husband, and at the same time assured her that nothing could exceed the favorable impression she had made on the young gentleman as well as on his father. This was all very perplexing. Events were crowding into the new sphere in which she had entered, and it seemed as if she was losing her footing, and was

carried on against her will into a course of du-
plicity. Silence was every moment binding her,
in a certain sense, to her present position as
Lady Davenant's daughter, and made a subsequent explanation more difficult. She felt it
absolutely necessary to make an effort to see
Joan Porter; yet at that moment her courage
to seek that interview almost failed her. The
hours that had elapsed since her arrival in London had displayed before her all the attractions
of the world, and the promenade in St. James's
Park left an impression on her mind, if not on
her heart, which the knowledge she had acquired
of its relation to her future destiny had not
tended to weaken. Everything combined to
lend an irresistible charm to her present position; everything except a sense of security and
the approval of her conscience. However, the
very desire to put an end to these painful doubts,
and make sure of her brilliant prospects, made
her feel the necessity of bringing the matter to
an issue, and at last she summoned resolution to
ask Lady Davenant if she might go and call on
her old friends. No objection was made on that

lady's part. She was expecting visits and did
not intend to drive out herself that day, but
said that Rose should take an airing, and might
go to Paddington as well as anywhere else.
The coach was ordered after dinner, and a
waiting-woman appointed to accompany Miss
Davenant to the cottage where she had spent
her childhood and her holidays whilst at
school. Mrs. Coggle was pleased and surprised to see a fine equipage stop at her door,
and did not at first see who was inside of it.
But when the young lady sprang out, and
running into the house, came into the parlor
and affectionately saluted her, she uttered an
exclamation of surprise, not unmixed with
consternation.

"How is Joan?" was her visitor's first question.

"Not by any means well, Miss Davenant;
much the reverse; indeed she is exceedingly
sick, and has not left her bed for several
weeks."

"I thought there was something amiss that
she did not come to Richmond. I am so

grieved—my own dear good Joan. I will go up at once to her, Coggy."

"Stop a bit, mistress; stop a bit. With whom have you come here?"

"With Lady Davenant's waiting-woman, and in her coach. She carried me away from school yesterday and brought me to her house in town."

"You had better not go upstairs then, my dear; and indeed, if I were you, I would get into the coach again and go back to where you came from."

"Without seeing Joan—my own dear Joan, and she so sick too! What can you be thinking of, Coggy?"

"More than you know of," was the oracular answer. Then, in an emphatic whisper, "There is some one upstairs!"

"Mrs. Yates?"

"Yes, indeed, Miss Davenant, her very self."

There are moments in life when the past and its memories, the present and its complications, the future and its possibilities, concentrate themselves in our minds with a startling clearness

and an almost intolerable keenness. Such was
the instant in which Rose or Mary, whichever
she was, heard the announcement that the person whom Joan had always told her was her
mother actually was in the house, and that in
another instant she should see her. The whole
importance of this crisis in her fate rushed upon
her. The very excess of feeling seemed to
paralyze feeling. She stood for a while motionless, as if on the brink of a precipice, with the
consciousness that the next step she took would
lead to safety or destruction. It was still in her
power to follow Mrs. Coggle's advice; to leave
the house, get into the coach, where the lady's-
maid was waiting for her, drive back to Davenant House, assume once for all, in heart as in
appearance, the position she occupied there, and
turn a deaf ear to all suggestions to the contrary. That was one obvious course, and a
tempting one to the weak side of a young girl's
heart. She saw in it a most alluring vista of
enjoyment and of future happiness; nor was it
unnatural, under the circumstances, that the
image of the young gentleman who had taken

such pains to insure a favorable reception for
the intelligence that had been communicated to
her a few hours ago, should be mixed up in that
rapid review of the importance of the ensuing
hour to the whole course of her life. This very
fact, however, armed her against her own weak-
ness. Truth, fidelity, and conscience cried out
against the suggestions of selfishness and vanity,
and the influence of a recent fancy. With the
doubt in her heart, if, indeed, it could be called
a doubt as to her birth, could she at once accept
as her mother the gay, the wealthy Lady Davenant, and forsake Mrs. Yates in her poverty
and sorrow? Could she, a Catholic—for never
had she in her heart denied her faith—throw in
her lot amongst Protestants, when she still
could hope to be the child of a Catholic? No,
she would not, she could not choose the crown
of flowers and refuse the crown of thorns. In
one of Mrs. Yates's letters allusion had been
made to this choice once offered to a saint. It
came to her mind then, as so many things do
in the course of a minute; she thought also
of some words she had read in a French book

at school, and had told Bessie Fairchild she would take as her motto, "Fais ce que dois, advienne que pourra," and leaving Mrs. Coggle in a very agitated state, she slowly but steadily walked up the stairs leading to Joan's room.

CHAPTER XIII.

JOAN PORTER'S ROOM.

THE door of the sick-chamber was open, and
this was the picture that met the visitor's eyes.
Her dear old friend was lying on the bed, with
the hue of death on her face, a calm, holy expression enlightening her plain, homely features, and
a crucifix in her hands, on which her eyes fixed
themselves with unspeakable love. By her side
sat one who had undergone much sorrow; one
who, though not old in years, was wan and gray-
haired; one dressed in a rusty black dress, that
hung loosely about her emaciated form. But
O, that woman's face! What a strange, heavenly
beauty was shining in its faded lineaments—the
beauty of a soul that had fought its way to peace
through many tribulations. Her eyes were the
very counterpart of the eyes which were at that
moment brimming full of tears—those of the
young girl who stood at the threshold of that

sick chamber. They were the same in color,
the same in expression, the same in melting tenderness. They looked at each other—that
woman and that girl. In the pale cheeks of the
one a faint color rose, whilst a deep flush over-
spread the face and brow of the other. Joan
had glanced at the door, and an exclamation
burst from her lips.

"Polly!" she cried; "your Polly!"

Mrs. Yates stood up trembling, restrained
from moving by the timidity of intense feeling.
In another moment Joan felt her darling's arms
round her neck, her tears falling on her face, and
words of love breathed in her ears.

"Stop, dear, stop," Joan whispered. "Don't
think of me now. That's your mother; kneel,
and ask her blessing."

Mrs. Yates hid her face in her hands, and
prayed inwardly for composure.

Polly—in Joan Porter's room we cannot call
her Rose—again threw her arms round Joan,
and said,

"Are you certain she is my mother?"

"Polly, dear, on the crucifix I swear she is,"

was the old woman's reply, and she laid her shrivelled hand on the sacred image.

The next moment Mrs. Yates was pressing to her heart her Mary, and thanking God for her recovered treasure. But quickly subduing her emotion, she said,

" Dear child, you are dressed like the daughter of wealthy parents. You have been acknowledged and claimed, I hear, by one who believes herself to be your mother. Is it from her house you come?"

"Yes, and she is very kind to me. But I never felt as if I was her child. And now even if Joan was not so sure of it, I *know* I am yours. I know it, mother; I feel it— deep, deep in my heart. O, put your hand on my head and bless me. Mother, I love you."

Who can measure the joy of the woman's heart who recovers her child? What must heaven be if earth has hours of such ecstasy as filled the soul of that mother who, after years of patient endurance, had her meed when she heard those words from her daughter's lips?

But one thought above all others was uppermost even then. She subdued her emotion. She looked earnestly at the agitated face of the young girl, and said,

"Mary, you know what it is to be a Catholic in this country. You know that I have no home to offer you but a poor garret, where I work for my bread since I came out of prison. Are you prepared to share my poverty—to lead the life our Blessed Lord and His Holy Mother led on earth, and serve God together in a Catholic manner, even unto suffering persecution for justice' sake?"

There was no mistaking the Ruth-like expression with which the answer to this question was given.

"I am prepared, mother, to live, to suffer, and to die with you." Then she drew from her bosom the crucifix which had been to her the visible symbol of her faith and the memorial of her absent mother since the day when she remembered Joan's first teaching her to kiss it. Mrs. Yates's tears flowed more freely at the sight of that little cross than they had yet done,

and for a while little was said by any one in that
room that could be written down; nothing but
prayers and loving exclamations, mingled with
kisses and broken sobs.

At last Mrs. Coggle came upstairs, and with
a vague sense that something was going on in
Joan's room to which she did not wish to be a
party one way or the other, she stood outside
the door and said,

" The lady that is in the coach says it is getting late and beginning to rain, and wishes
Miss Davenant to know that her mamma will
be soon wanting her at home."

This message broke the charm of the first
moments of recognition, and awoke Mrs. Yates
and her daughter to the difficulties of their
position. Neither of them had the shadow of
a doubt as to the fact of their relationship, but
how to establish it, how to state it to Lady
Davenant, how to act if she refused to listen to
them, was beyond their power at that moment
to conceive. They were, in truth, three very
helpless creatures—a poor dying woman, a
friendless one just liberated from a long impris-

onment, and one who three days before was a mere school-girl.

" Must I go? must I leave you, mother? I will do what you tell me."

Mrs. Yates thought, or rather prayed, for a moment, and then said, " I know not how to proceed, save by simply speaking the truth, and leaving to God the rest. I know but of one friend in the world who would, perhaps, help me to convince Lady Davenant. That is Sir Mark Le Grange, by whose means, through dear Joan's recourse to him, I got out of prison.

Mary, for so we must now call her, blushed at the mention of Sir Mark's name. She had told Mrs. Yates of her removal from school to London and of the kindness of Lady Davenant, but had not adverted to an incident of the last eventful days which might have made her feel as if some sort of sacrifice besides that of a wealthy parentage had been made by her child.

" Have you courage," Mrs. Yates asked, " to go back to Lady Davenant and tell her the whole truth?"

" More courage than to spend another day in

her house without doing so. Perhaps she will be quite willing to give me up to you when she hears what no one has yet told her."

"I did write to her more than ônce," Joan said, in a feeble voice. "It took me many hours each time, and a heavy postage besides. But my letters never do reach them as they are written to."

This was not very unaccountable, considering the peculiarities of Joan's spelling and her ideas of geography. The letters to Lady Davenant had been directed to "Mount Pellew, beyond seas," and were, no doubt, lying at some post-office in a seaport town of France or Belgium.

"If Lady Davenant should be angry, and refuse to believe or examine into what I shall tell her, how shall I act, dear mother?"

"You must then be patient and wait, my loved one. I have a firm trust that God will make manifest the truth, so that we shall not be forever parted. My Mary, I would offer, when once truth and justice are satisfied by a statement of the real facts to that good lady, to resign you to her, if such should be her wish and yours. But I dare not do so, for I know that the interests of your soul would be in danger. She can give you everything this world can bestow. For a few years she can make your life a round of pleasure, but when this brief space of time is passed, what will wealth and pleasure then avail? O my child, what shall a man give in exchange for his soul?"

"Mother, my mind is made up. Nothing but force or your own commands shall keep me apart from you. You know I have loved you since I could speak, and that I have never believed I was Lady Davenant's daughter."

"She will be as bad as the woman who wanted to cut the child in two," Joan ejaculated, "if she does not give you back to your own mother, and she just come out of prison! Tell her a dying woman says so."

"No, no, dear Joan," Mrs. Yates whispered. "Judge not hardly of her; she may well struggle against the truth that takes away from her her life's joy."

"I don't think one bit that she cares that much about Polly. Why did she not come from France long ago for to see her, if she had a mother's heart? But God forgive her and me too, if I am wanting in charity. But you see, Mrs. Yates, I have had to fight a battle with her all through, though she did not know it."

Another knock, and Mrs. Coggle's voice at the door startled them all. This time she put in her head and said,

"The lady in the coach is half demented with impatience; she says her lady will be out of her mind if she is not at home in time to dress her for the play."

Roused by this second warning, Mrs. Yates and her daughter rose hastily.

"See, my child," the former said, "this is a letter I wrote last night to Lady Davenant. Give it to her at a favorable moment, and await what she will say. If she shows herself willing to examine into the truth of what I have written, and is not angered by it, then show her this medallion, which contains my picture when I was about your present age. The likeness to yourself is so great that I think it would carry conviction to any mind fairly inclined."

" And tell her," Joan added, " that a Christian woman, now on her death-bed, is ready to take her oath before she goes to meet her Judge that you are Mary Yates, whom we always called Polly."

Thus armed, thus instructed, and thus blest by two anxious, loving hearts, Mary went her way.   The waiting-woman was loud in her complaints of the length of the visit, and expressed fears of her mistress's displeasure. Lady Davenant was indeed seated at her toilet table when they arrived, and company waiting in the drawing-room to accompany her to the play.   She did not, however, show any ill-humor to her dear Rose, and asked if she would like to accompany her to the theatre.   But when she prayed to be excused on the score of a headache, which was indeed no counterfeit, she readily consented to her staying at home, and advised her to lie down and entertain herself with the translation of the great " Cyrus," Mdlle. de Scudery's last romance.

" To-morrow," she added, " I am to sit early for my picture, and then shall have twenty visits to return. You are paler than when you went out to-day," she remarked. "The air of Paddington has done you no good. If your complexion is habitually so pale, you must wear rouge. I will show you myself how to put it on. Poor little Rose," she said, kissing her forehead, "we must make you a damask rose—not so poor a white one as you look to-day."

All this was very kind; but fresh from the atmosphere of Joan's room, Mary Yates felt an emotion of joy at the thought that this gay and lovely lady, amiable and charming as she was, was not her mother.

It was not till the next day was far advanced that an opportunity offered for the performance of the duty which she had to discharge. When at last she found herself alone with Lady Davenant, each occupied with some light fancy work, she said to herself, "Now or never; it must be done;" and drawing Mrs. Yates's letter from her bosom, she presented it to her with these words:

"Madam, a lady whom I saw yesterday at Paddington begged me to give this letter into

your hands. It contains somewhat of great
consequence to you, dear lady, and to my poor
self. Will you read it?"

"Good heavens, child! What's the matter?
Your heart seems very full. Tears! Poor little soul! What can it be all about?"

"You will know, dear madam, when you have
read that letter."

Lady Davenant broke the seal and glanced
at the signature.

"Mary Yates! that is the name of the widow
of poor George Yates! Sir Mark Le Grange
told me yesterday she was released from prison
through his efforts. How came you to have
been charged with this letter, Rose?"

"Read it, madam, and you will see how
nearly it concerns me."

"Concerns you? I should like to know what
can concern a child like you, except some new
trinkets, or a school-fellow's visit. By the way,
when will your friend Bessie Fairchild's holidays begin?"

"O madam, do read the letter." A burst of
tears accompanied the words.

With more curiosity than any other feeling, Lady Davenant began to read.

"It is no doubt," she thought, "a petition for assistance. Sir Mark said she was destitute. Most gladly will I give it, for I have often felt troubled at the fate of those poor people."

In no ill-disposed mood she perused Mrs. Yates's appeal.

CHAPTER XIV.

THE MOTHER'S APPEAL.

MRS. YATES's letter to Lady Davenant was as follows:

"MADAM AND HONORED COUSIN,—My name and parentage are not unknown to you, for the husband whom it hath pleased the Almighty some years back to take from me was Mr. George Yates, a nephew of the late Mr. Mordaunt. He hath often spoken to me in our happy by-gone days of your kind behavior toward him when he had the honor of meeting you at his uncle's house. Your ladyship is no doubt aware of the motives which induced Mr. Mordaunt to banish from his presence one whom he had once fondly regarded, and who had committed no fault in his eyes except that which he could not omit without imperilling his soul. His subsequent marriage to one of the same faith as himself enhanced and confirmed this displeasure, and no reconciliation between them was ever effected. Whilst lamenting this estrangement, my husband often rejoiced that his uncle, for whom he entertained the most affectionate sentiments, though conscientious differences had parted them from each other, enjoyed the society and the filial care of so good a kinswoman as your ladyship.

"My own history has been marked by a number of successive troubles, beginning with my husband's declining health, suddenly aggravated by a hasty flight beyond seas on the night of the Fire of London, and his death two years afterwards in an obscure village of France. But, madam, that hasty flight, caused by the dangers which accrued to recusants in consequence of the suspicion which fell at that time on Catholics, of having been concerned

in a plot to bring about that great public calamity, was the cause
of another heavy grief to me. I was forced to leave in London
our little daughter, then only three weeks old. One Mrs. Coggle, well known to your ladyship, received her from me on that
memorable night, and Joan Porter, her servant and a humble
friend of my family, promised me to be a good friend to my poor
child, and that promise has been well kept. But, madam, here
is the strange part of the story. On the same night, after I had
left the house, it was permitted by Divine Providence that another
infant, rather by accident than through design, was left on their
hands; and subsequently a dispute arose between Mrs. Coggle
and her servant as to which of the two children was mine, the
other having been thrown out of a window of a house which is
supposed to have been Davenant House.

"When, after my husband's death, I returned to London, at first
I could not discover whither the good woman who had charge
of my child had removed; but meeting by accident in the
streets Joan Porter, she gave me their address, and in a somewhat
urgent manner pressed me to lose no time in claiming my little
girl. I was in as great a hurry to do so as she could be, and said
I should go to the house that day as soon as I had discharged a
trust that had been committed to me by one to whom I had great
obligations. In the performance of this sacred duty I fell into the
hands of the pursuivants, and was thrown into prison, where I
remained ten long years, during the first three of which I had no
means of informing Joan Porter where I was. At last a message
reached her, and from time to time she sent me tidings of my
daughter. Then I learnt that, against her will and constant prot-
estation, Mrs. Coggle had given your ladyship to understand that
my little Mary was the child which had been saved from the fire at
Davenant House, and brought to her house by a poor neighbor, and
never told you that, on the same night, I left my child with her,
or giving you an opportunity of speaking with Joan, who would
have told you that the infant whose parents were unknown had
died on her knees at the age of about two years, after having been
conditionally baptized. I accuse not Mrs. Coggle's motives, or

question her belief in what she asserted; yet I doubt if she would take her oath of it, as Joan Porter, who is now near unto death, will readily do, that the young girl you look upon as your own daughter, and have taken into your house as Rose Davenant, is no other than my own child, Mary Yates.

"This, madam, is the plain unvarnished statement which I place before you; weigh it carefully before God, and may He guide you to a right conclusion! You have played a generous mother's part toward this child. You have been at the pains and expense of her maintenance and education; and, without requiring more absolute proofs than such as satisfied your heart, you have taken her to your bosom. For my part, I have none to offer which the law would admit of, even if an all but outlawed and very poor creature could gain a hearing. It is one woman's word against another; it is one fond and yearning mother's heart pleading against another as fond and yearning perhaps as her own. In the world's estimation I should be acting a kind part toward her whom you call Rose, and who is my Mary, if I was to leave her in your ladyship's hands without a struggle to regain her, and withdraw myself to some shelter, so as to be never heard of again. But neither toward God, nor toward you, nor toward her, should I thus discharge my duty. This is not the only world we have to think of. Life is short and eternity long. We have each but one soul, and what can a man give in exchange for his soul? What will it avail us to have gained the whole world should we lose it, and fail in that for which we were created?

"Believing, as I do most firmly, that this young girl is my daughter, I have no choice left but on my knees, Lady Davenant, to beseech you to restore her to me. She is willing to share my poverty, and I have that to share with her which is beyond all earthly treasures. Do you think that one situated as I am would try to take your child from you, if she was not convinced that it is her own that she asks for? O, dear honored lady, look at the picture which, when you have perused this, will be placed in your hands. It was an exact likeness of me before age and sorrow had changed my appearance. See if it does not bear a striking con-

formity to her who is Rose to you and Mary to me.   Come, then,
and hear from Joan Porter's dying lips her solemn asseveration
of what I assert.   Mrs. Coggle will not, I think, venture on her
oath to deny it, and then you will decide.   Believe me, with a
very full heart and tender feelings toward one who has loved
and befriended *that* child whom I believe to be my own,
    "Your ladyship's humble and obedient servant,
                                        "MARY YATES."

Lady Davenant's color had risen whilst she
read this letter.   When she had finished it, she
said in a cold manner:

"Do you yourself think that you are this
person's daughter, and not mine?"

"I do, madam; because Joan Porter, from
the earliest time I can remember, told me I was
Mrs. Yates's child."

Lady Davenant started.

"Indeed; and why was I not told so?"

"Mrs. Coggle said the contrary; and when
you came to fetch me, and no doubt was
expressed by yourself or Mrs. Dimple that I
was your daughter, I had not courage to speak.
I did not know if it would be right to do so."

"Where is the picture this letter speaks
of?"

After looking at it fixedly, and then at the

downcast face before her, Lady Davenant's eyes filled with tears.

"It is a horrid disappointment," she exclaimed. "And it's so hard upon you," she added; "such a change in your prospects."

"It would be very hard indeed, if I was not allowed to love you still," Mary Yates said, and burst into tears.

There was more tenderness in the embrace that followed this speech than in any caress hitherto exchanged between her and Lady Davenant.

The rest of the evening passed uneasily for both of them. They did not speak farther of the subject that was uppermost in their minds, and to speak of anything else seemed impossible.

Lady Davenant never closed her eyes during the night, and went through a variety of emotions and phases of feeling. At first she felt discomposed, even angry, and inclined to treat Mrs. Yates's statement with contempt, and said to herself that Joan Porter, whoever she was, might be a half-witted simpleton. But still she could not but see that Mrs. Yates's letter was not that of an impostor or a fool, and the likeness between her portrait and Rose was too remarkable to be overlooked. It had indeed always struck her that there was not the slightest resemblance between her and any one of her own family; and when she came to think of it, she was not only very much like Mrs. Yates's picture, but there was something in the expression of her countenance which strongly reminded her of George Yates. The more she dwelt on the coincidences the case presented, the less could she doubt as to the facts they pointed to. The first effect of this dawning conviction was to irritate her usually smooth temper. All sorts of unamiable and angry feelings rose in her mind.

"Very well, be it so. I have been cruelly deceived, and I shall have nothing more to say to any of them. If this ungrateful girl prefers to be the daughter of an obscure recusant, to the position that was destined for her, she may please herself; I shall not stand in the way."

In this mood she tried to compose herself to

sleep, but in vain. From under her pillow she took Mrs. Yates's letter, and by the aid of the rush-light again read it through. There were words in it that seemed written in fiery characters : " What shall a man give in exchange for his soul? Life and eternity, heaven and hell." Those were thoughts which she had put away from her, which she had never suffered her mind to dwell on since the days when she had learnt the catechism at her mother's knee. Had that mother prayed in heaven, and obtained that an angel messenger should be sent that night to her child? Like so many in those days, Lady Davenant had been baptized a Catholic, and brought up one till her mother died. Afterwards she had conformed to the times; never occupied herself much with religion; hardened her heart against occasional flashes of remorse or desire for better things, and so lived on in careless unconcern. But that night a sudden change—one of those sudden revolutions which sometimes come over a soul, upheaving the memories of the past, and throwing a strange light on the future—took place within her. It so happened that Sir Mark Le Grange, a good man in his way, had spoken to her the day before of that very Mary Yates, in a way which he little dreamed would make upon her the impression which it did. He happened to be the person who, through some friends, Joan Porter had contrived to interest in behalf of the neglected and forgotten prisoner. It was to his efforts that her release had been owing. He was pleased with his achievement, and liked to talk of it. " These poor Papists," he had said to Lady Davenant, "are strange people. As a magistrate I had frequent access to that Mrs. Yates, previous to her release. Upon my word, madam, she surprised me. One would have thought she was in possession of some great secret happiness, her countenance was so serene and contented. Catholics have, I take it, strange ideas with regard to sufferings, which help to confirm them in their recusancy. This lady told me that if she had not a child, and therefore a duty to perform in the world, she should have asked no better than to spend the remainder of her life in gaol; and I believe she was speaking the truth. I never met with a woman of a more forcible and at the same time sweet a spirit."

These words, which did not make much impression on Lady Davenant at the time, returned to her recollection during the sleepless hours of the long night. They confirmed her belief in Mrs. Yates's statement, and awakened thoughts of what her own life had been during all the years that patient captive had spent in prison. The more she dwelt on this contrast, the more deeply it affected her. Grace was at work in a heart long closed to its influence. Under the gilded canopy of a bed which was wetted with her tears, a new life was beginning for Lady Davenant. Faint as the first morning light after a dark night, that gleam of faith shone on her soul. If the pale watcher by Joan Porter's sick couch could have seen her trying to pray, she would have felt repaid for all she had suffered. Could she have seen the progress and end of what was begun that night, how deep would have been her joy!

CHAPTER XV.

ROSEMARY.

EARLY in the morning a loud knock was heard at the door of Mrs. Coggle's house, and when it was opened a person stepped in, whom she admitted without any remark or question. He knew his way upstairs, and went at once into the room where Joan was lying. Mrs. Yates had arranged a little altar, and prepared, as well as under the circumstances was possible, for the reception of Him who was coming to visit and bless His aged servant. Joan had made an effort to sit up in her bed, and a gleam of joy lighted up her features when the priest came in. She lifted up her feeble hand and made the sign of the cross. After depositing the Blessed Sacrament on the little altar, he bent over the dying woman to hear her whispered confession. It was a short one, for he had seen her two days before. After giving her absolution, he was adding a few fervent words of consolation, when the door of the room was gently opened, and two persons with their faces veiled came in, and knelt behind the curtain at the foot of the bed. Mrs. Yates gave an anxious glance at the priest, and then at Joan, who was absorbed in prayer, and had not noticed the entrance of these strangers. He stood still an instant, as if hesitating how to act; then crossing the room, he said, in a low voice, to the two kneeling persons,

"Are you both Catholics?"

One of those he thus addressed lifted up her veil, and looking at him with streaming eyes, answered,

"O Father Levison, I am one, though unworthy of the name. It was you who instructed me for my first communion; and this child, whether she is mine or no, is a child of the Church: suffer us, I beseech you, to remain here."

The priest bowed his head in token of assent; and after kneeling an instant before the Blessed Sacrament, he carried it to Joan. She received her Lord as those receive Him who through life have always looked forward to death as the messenger of God's love. Her homely features were lighted up with an expression of strange beauty, a look of unutterable joy beamed in her dying eyes, a smile hovered on her lips, and for a while she remained silent and motionless in communion with her God. Not a sound disturbed the stillness of the chamber, where at that moment many ardent prayers were addressed to Him whose nearness was felt by all present. Joan herself was the first to speak. She called the priest, and said,

"I am very happy, Father, but very, very weak. Do you think that lady will come? I was praying just now not to die before I could speak to her."

"If you mean Lady Davenant, I think she is here," he answered. "It will be well that you should bear witness before her and Mrs. Yates to the fact that so nearly concerns them. They have both been present during your communion. I will call them to your side."

A moment afterwards the two mothers whose

histories had been so strangely connected, and the young girl whom each had looked upon as her child, stood by Joan Porter's side. Mrs. Coggle placed herself behind them, in a state of painful bewilderment. She was broken-hearted at Joan's condition ; remorseful at her long neglect of her faith, which the solemn act she had just witnessed had revived in her heart ; distressed at a few words that Lady Davenant had said to her before she had entered the sick chamber, implying that she had been deceived ; to which was superadded a vague sense that her conduct in all that business had not been irreproachable, and that Joan might, after all, have been the best informed on the subject.

It was with intense emotion that the witnesses of that scene, in which they were all so deeply interested, saw Father Levison place in Joan's hands the crucifix, which she devoutly kissed, and then breathlessly listened to the words she uttered in a feeble but distinct voice,

"As I hope to be saved, and as I am about for to appear before my God, I do say, and am sure of it, that this child on whom I lay my hand is the one Mrs. Yates left in my arms on the night of the Fire of London, and I pray God she may be restored to her."

After a brief and solemn pause, which followed this declaration, Lady Davenant came forward, and, taking Joan's hand she said, " After reading Mrs. Yates's statement, I was wellnigh convinced of what you have now affirmed. Since I have seen her in this room, by the side of—*her* daughter, for such I must now call her—no doubt can remain. Mrs. Coggle's embarrassed replies to my questions and your testimony were scarce needed to assure me of the truth."

Joan feebly pressed the hand that held hers, and sighed as if a heavy load was removed from her heart. There was another pause, during which Mrs. Yates passed her arm around her daughter's waist, and drew her close to herself, and Mrs. Coggle left the room, puzzled as to her own position at that moment, and ready to accuse or defend herself as would please every one most. Lady Davenant was still holding Joan's hand, and seemed unwilling to move. Bending over her, she whispered in a trembling voice, " The other child—*my* child, Joan ! She died, then ?"

" Yes, my lady, her little soul went to heaven white from its baptism, and here, under my pillow—get out that little parcel, Polly, and give it to the lady."

With trembling hands, Lady Davenant opened the parcel, a mass of delicate silken and very fair hair met her sight.

The mother's heart was wakened then. She pressed it to her lips and to her bosom, and bedewed it with her tears. It was what she could well imagine her child's hair to have been.

" God bless you !" she said to Joan. " Pray for me." And then whispered to the priest as she left the room, " I would fain be reconciled, Father. Take me where I can confess, and at your feet promise to lead henceforward a Catholic life."

She kept her word. Sudden had been the work of conversion in her soul, but it proved a lasting one—one of those rare miracles of grace which occur now and then to teach us never to

doubt the power of prayer. She had been hard
and cold and worldly for many years, no refreshing dew had moistened her soul; no light from
heaven had shone on her path. Many there are
who feed on husks, because they have missed
the road to their Father's house. She, that
apparently heartless woman, had found the
way to it that day, and with it the lost treasures of Faith, Hope, and Love. She forgave
the poor woman who had scarcely consciously
deceived her, and provided for her old age.
Sweetly and urgently she invited Mrs. Yates to
her house, pleading for a share in her child's
affection. Mrs. Yates accepted the offer for a
a time, Father Levison having urged it upon
her as the greatest benefit that could be con-
ferred on the new convert. It was with a full
heart and streaming eyes that she placed her
daughter's hand in Lady Davenant's and said,

"You have a claim on her equal to mine,
sweet lady. She shall no more be called Rose
or Mary, but Rose-Mary; and may she repay
you, if only one half of the goodness you have
shown her!"

Davenant House soon possessed a little secret chapel, which became a frequent resort for Catholics. Many Masses were said in it for the repose of the soul of Joan Porter, who breathed her last a few hours after that communion which had been the means of Lady Davenant's conversion. Rosemary wept bitterly for her old friend. Not all the love of her two mothers consoled her for a time for the loss of one who had truly been a parent to her. After her death, the virtues of this humble servant of God became yet more apparent than in life, and some affirmed that she died in the odor of sanctity. Lady Davenant placed a memorial of her in the same place where, at the foot of the Crucifix, was enshrined the fair hair of the child who had died on her knees. In this hidden sanctuary Mrs. Yates poured forth many prayers that the time might come when, withdrawing herself entirely from the world, she might resume that life of silent contemplation and prayer which she had learnt to prize during her long imprisonment.

One day, toward the close of the year, Lady

Davenant received a letter which, after she had read it, she gave with a smile to Mrs. Yates.

" Dear friend," she said, " the ways of Providence are passing strange! What would have naturally wrecked many a hope of the sort will prove, I think, a stepping-stone to a happy issue." This enigmatical speech was explained by the letter which follows:

" HONORED AND DEAR MADAM,—You are well aware how strongly my desires were set on the union which had been treated of between us, and how greatly confirmed they were, which were so strong already, by the sight of your amiable and accomplished daughter, who unites in herself all that birth, parentage, and personal merit of person and of mind can be desired or imagined. I may add, that my son was likewise so impressed with admiration and a very tender sentiment of esteem for the young lady, with whom he had the happiness of conversing at some length on the day when we were kindly entertained in your house, that he would have thought himself the happiest of men to have obtained her hand and merited your approbation. But in this world the best feelings of our nature, and even the generosity of youthful ardor in what touches conscience, sometimes militates against the best-contrived schemes and blights the fairest hopes.

" Madam, it is with the deepest regret I find that, whereas I have always judged it to be my duty to conform to the religion by law established in this kingdom, as sufficient for any Christian man, and the most convenient for a dutiful subject of this realm —in which sentiments I know you concur with me—my son, now that he has come of age, refuses to do so, and—with a fanatical attachment to the worship of the Church of Rome, wherein he was educated by a mother, of which her religion was the only defect—persists in his recusancy, and writes to me from abroad, that although he never met with any one he admired or could love so well as Miss Davenant, he will neither conceal his sentiments nor marry one who is not Catholic. I have by letter reasoned with him, but in vain. He alleges the interests of his conscience and the importance of his soul in comparison with the world's fortune, and by many virtuous reasons seeks to justify an undutiful resolve. At the same time, he is so good and tender a son, and owes so much to a mother whose memory I likewise worship, that I find it difficult to speak harshly of his conduct; and if he chooses to lead a private life, and marry one of his own religion, I cannot quarrel with him, though my paternal affection grieves at his resolution. Your daughter will find many suitors more noble, more wealthy, than my poor son, but none who, but for this untoward circumstance, would have devoted his life more faithfully to her service and happiness.

"I remain, dear and honored madam, your faithful, humble, and obedient servant,

"MARK LE GRANGE, BART."

"Dear cousin," Lady Davenant said, when Mrs. Yates returned to her this letter, "Mary Yates will have the same portion that was promised with Rose Davenant. So I think this good gentleman will be satisfied to receive our little recusant as his daughter-in-law; and if you had seen the sudden admiration his son conceived for Rose-Mary, and her good opinion of him in return, you would anticipate, as I do,

that when these young people become acquaint-
ed with their reciprocal sentiments regarding
their souls' welfare and God's Holy Church,
they will be overjoyed and ready to fulfil the
contract passed betwixt Sir Mark and myself.
Ah, dear friend, if this marriage takes place,
you and I will seek together other nuptials, and
end our lives in a different manner from what
we should have forecasted on the night of the
Fire of London!"

Six months afterwards Mary Yates was united
to the son and heir of Sir Mark Le Grange,
and her two mothers entered the convent of
Poor Clares at Gravelines—Mrs. Yates with
the sober and deep devotion of a long-tried
and delayed vocation, Lady Davenant with
the ardent fervor of one who loved much,
because she had to make up to the Heart of
our Divine Lord for years of cold neglect and
sinful estrangement. They ran henceforward
a close and devout race in the narrow path
of Christian perfection. They were lovely in
their lives, and in their deaths they were not
divided.

www.ingramcontent.com/pod-product-compliance
Lightning Source LLC
Chambersburg PA
CBHW022354020726

47500CB00002B/271